ID0397031

SUNSHINE

Bauer, Marion Dane, author.
Sunshine

2021
33305251920413
sa   05/28/21

SUNSHINE

Marion Dane Bauer

CANDLEWICK PRESS

This is a work of fiction. Names, characters, places, and incidents are either products of the author's imagination or, if real, are used fictitiously.

Copyright © 2021 by Marion Dane Bauer

All rights reserved. No part of this book may be reproduced, transmitted, or stored in an information retrieval system in any form or by any means, graphic, electronic, or mechanical, including photocopying, taping, and recording, without prior written permission from the publisher.

First edition 2021

Library of Congress Catalog Card Number pending
ISBN 978-1-5362-1411-6

21 22 23 24 25 26 LBM 10 9 8 7 6 5 4 3 2 1

Printed in Melrose Park, IL, USA

This book was typeset in Goudy Old Style.

Candlewick Press
99 Dover Street
Somerville, Massachusetts 02144

www.candlewick.com

A JUNIOR LIBRARY GUILD SELECTION

For my granddaughter,
Bailey Dane Bataille,
who will know why.
And in memory of Dawn,
the real-life model for Sunshine.

Chapter 1
Very Glad to Meet You

"Is that her?"

Ben sits on the edge of the dock, shading his eyes to peer across the lake. He points to a narrow silver object poised on the water far away and asks again, "Is that my mother?"

"Hope so." His father settles next to him onto the dock, his dangling feet reaching almost to the slapping gray water. "Your mom said noon and it's past that now."

"But you said she'd come in a boat," Ben objects. "That's a canoe."

His father zips his jacket against the cool breeze

riffling across the lake. Early June so far north in Minnesota barely qualifies as summer. "A canoe *is* a boat," he says.

Ben wrinkles his nose. When he heard *boat*, he'd dreamed of a speedboat. Something that would go fast. Something that wouldn't need paddling.

Still . . . it's his mother. And she's coming.

He leans as far forward as he can without losing his balance. If he can't speed her up, he'll come as close as he can from his side. It's been so long since he's seen her. So very long. He can barely remember what she looks like.

She's sure going to be glad to see me, Sunshine. I know she will.

Ben doesn't give voice to the words. He doesn't need to. His little dog hears his every thought.

Casually, so as not to call attention to what he's doing, he drops his hand to Sunshine's soft fur. Then he looks down, startled. His hand rests on the rough boards of the dock. Sunshine isn't there!

Where is she? He's been so excited about seeing his mother, he's forgotten her entirely. Has he thought about her even once since they got out of the car?

As always happens, though, the instant he calls her to mind, Sunshine is there. Not next to him this time, but running toward him down the rickety dock.

Her long ears fly. Her reddish-gold fur gleams. Her paws splay happily in every direction.

The sight of that galumphing run warms Ben's belly.

Sunshine slides to a stop next to him, plops her butt down, and smiles her sweet doggy smile. *Don't worry,* the smile says. *I'm here. You know I'm always here!*

Ben lays a hand on her hard little skull and goes back to watching the approaching canoe. He can make out the paddler now. Or at least he can make out a baseball cap and a green shirt.

Sunshine leans into him, and Ben can't help himself. He bends over to kiss her wet black nose.

"You're doing it again, aren't you?" his father says.

Ben jerks upright. His father is studying him, his usually friendly face pulled tight with some idea he doesn't like.

"Doing what?" Ben widens his eyes.

His father doesn't answer. He just shakes his head and goes back to watching the canoe's progress.

Ben studies Dad's face. His cheeks are smoothly shaved and gleaming. He's a teacher, and ever since school let out he's been sprouting dark bristles. Which means he shaved for *her*. Ben loves knowing his father shaved for her. What he doesn't love is the way his father gets annoyed these days by everything having to do with Sunshine.

Sunshine settles, half sprawled across Ben's lap, and he closes a furry paw in his hand. He does it without looking down, though, keeping his eyes on the approaching canoe.

Sunshine licks the back of his hand.

They wait. All three of them wait. The canoe is moving so slowly.

His mother could hardly have gone farther away and still been in Minnesota. If the narrow road that brought them here had held out a few more miles, they could have driven right into Canada.

And she could hardly have found a quieter, more remote place. This town is so small, it hardly deserves to be called a town. Some tourist cabins and an old family resort scattered along the lakeshore, a general store that sells fishing tackle and bait and groceries, a gas station, a ramshackle motel and café, a few houses.

A fish leaps out of the water not far away. When it smacks back down, silvery spray spatters the dock.

"Hey!" his dad says. "That was a big one!"

Ben wonders why his father cares how big the fish is. He's not an outdoorsy guy. He's never once taken Ben fishing.

Ben kisses Sunshine's nose again, runs a hand along her back, stripping the wet from her fur.

Dad sighs and drapes an arm across Ben's shoulders. Ben ignores the familiar weight, the warmth. He concentrates instead on Sunshine, moving his hand from the top of her head to the tip of her long plumed tail in exaggerated sweeps.

"I'm not sure what your mother will think—" Dad starts to say.

Ben interrupts. "She knows about Sunshine, doesn't she? You've told her?" Surely they've talked about the "problem" of his dog during one of their phone conversations.

His father shakes his head.

Ben considers that. So she doesn't know. Well . . . okay. Then maybe her mind won't be made up.

What else does she not know about him? She probably doesn't know that sometimes he hangs around his friends' houses just to see if *their* mothers will notice him.

Dad has told him just about everything about her. That one day when he was only three years old, she left. Dad was off teaching, and she just walked out. She left everything, not just him and his dad. The city, her friends, her old life. And she moved up here to the wilderness. To live on an island. Alone.

You can't get much more alone than living on an island in the wilderness of northern Minnesota.

She doesn't spend her winters on the island, of course. When it gets cold, she moves to the resort near the town. The owners go off to Florida to get warm, and she takes care of the place through the long winter. As alone in the snow and cold as she is on the island.

And she never comes back to St. Paul. Not even to visit her son.

He knows, too, that she's a writer. She writes articles for magazines, brochures for resorts, stuff like that. He even knows that lately she's been working on a novel.

His father has told him all this, because Ben doesn't talk to her.

The truth is, he hasn't wanted to talk to her. He's not sure why. He just hasn't. At least not until now when he came up with his plan. But for his plan to work, they have to do more than talk. They have to see one another, get to know one another. He has to visit her on her island for a whole week.

Dad didn't like the idea at first. He said Ben hardly knew his mother. He said she lives too far away. He said she might not want to invite him.

Finally, he said he would ask.

And his mother said yes.

The mother he can barely remember said he could come visit.

He remembers a few things. Like the animal pancakes she used to make. Giraffes with endless necks, rabbits with enormous ears, elephants with trunks so long they dripped off the edge of the plate.

But he doesn't remember what she looks like.

You'd think Dad would have photos, but he doesn't. "Your mother hated having her picture taken," he says when Ben asks.

It won't matter now, though . . . photos or no photos. Because he's going to see the real thing. His real mother.

Ben's mouth has gone dry and his legs jitter. Only running his fingers through Sunshine's soft fur keeps him still. But despite Sunshine's fur, another worry tugs at him, the one that started up the moment the canoe came into view.

"I've never paddled a canoe," he says, his gaze on the sunlight flashing off his mother's paddle.

Dad's arm tightens around Ben's shoulders.

"You'll do fine," he says. "You won't be paddling alone. Besides, your mother will teach you."

"But what if it's far? What if my arms fall off before we get there?"

Dad tugs on one of Ben's arms. He grins. "Nope," he says, "not going to happen. Too well attached."

Ben grins, too. He can't help it.

But then his father adds softly, "You can change your mind, you know. You don't have to do this."

Ben shakes his head. Violently. Just because he's a little bit nervous doesn't mean he wants to change his mind.

"Then," his father says, his voice growing more firm, "no what-ifs. It's going to be fine."

Ben ducks his head to hide his burning face. *The what-if kid.* That's what Dad calls him sometimes. Because he's such a worrier.

His father is pretty patient with his what-ifs. He says things like *You'll get braver as you get bigger, Ben. I promise.*

But what if—he can't help it, there it is again—what if his mother can't stand a what-if kid?

The canoe has grown larger, the paddler more distinct. She's smallish. Didn't his mother used to be big? And the green shirt is plaid. But the low-riding baseball cap hides both face and hair.

Her strokes are steady and strong.

Ben closes his eyes. He opens them again. She's still coming.

When the canoe pulls up below him, next to the dock, he looks down at the long, shining braid emerging from the back of the cap and catches his breath.

His mother's hair is a rich reddish-gold. The same coppery sheen as Sunshine's fur. As if she knew about Sunshine, the Sunshine that Dad says he never told her about, and dyed her hair to match.

Sunshine isn't impressed with the match. She peers over the edge of the dock, the fur rising on the back of her neck. A growl rumbles beneath Ben's hand, so low he can feel rather than hear it.

He squeezes the back of her neck, and she stops.

When his mother looks up, though, Ben knows

the color is real, has always been real. Everything about her—the pale, freckled face; the slender, almost boyish form; the coppery hair . . . all of it is achingly familiar.

How can you forget somebody so completely and yet recognize every bit?

"Hello, Benny," she says.

The voice is lower, larger than the woman in the canoe.

Hello! his heart sings. *Hello! Hello!*

But his response, always his response when anyone calls him Benny, pops out before he can stop it. "I'm Ben, not Benny."

A flush climbs his mother's throat, stains her cheeks. She nods. "Ben it is, then. Hello, Ben."

He's sorry. So sorry. How could he start out so wrong? He and Sunshine both.

His mother tosses a rope and Dad catches it. Then in a move so swift Ben has no time to pre-pare, she vaults onto the dock . . . and lands so nearly on top of Sunshine that he cries out.

His little dog doesn't make a sound, though. She just walks away as if nothing has happened.

And Ben's mother stands there looking down at him, looking and looking.

He scrambles to his feet and holds out a hand. She takes it, her eyebrows arching in something like surprise.

"I'm very glad to meet you," he says.

His mother, the mother he has waited practically his whole life to see, tosses her head back and laughs.

CHAPTER 2
Yes!

Ben picks up a cold French fry, drops it under the table for Sunshine, then wipes his greasy fingers on his jeans.

He can't believe he said such a dumb thing.

To his own mother!

I'm very glad to meet you.

As though he didn't grow inside her the way babies do. As though she didn't take care of him every single day for more than three years.

No wonder she laughed.

At least he hasn't said anything else dumb.

When they first sat down, she asked the kinds of questions grown-ups always ask.

What's your favorite subject in school?

Recess.

Are you playing any sports?

Baseball. Except he's not playing baseball now. He's here.

When she ran out of questions, she couldn't seem to think of anything else to say. And despite all the things he'd wanted to talk to her about when he finally saw her, the conversations he made up every night lying in bed, he couldn't think of anything, either. All the topics he'd lined up in his head, the words he'd laid out, suddenly seemed silly.

But Dad isn't having any problem. He can think of all kinds of things to talk about, and she responds easily, leaving Ben squished into silence in a corner of the café booth.

They talk about people they both used to know, teachers at the high school, neighbors. Who has moved, who has retired, who has gotten a divorce or a baby. About "the state of the world," too. The state of the world makes them both sigh.

You'd think adults would take better care of the world so they wouldn't have to sigh about it so much.

Ben stares out the café window at the empty street. Not much to see out there. Sometimes a car goes by. A kid pedals past on a bicycle, but then the street is empty again.

Beyond the street are trees. Trees and trees and trees. And lakeshore. And the endless gray lake.

He leans back into the cushioned vinyl and drops into a story, the one he was building in the car.

It's an easy drop. Comforting. Like slipping into warm water.

Or like gathering Sunshine into his arms and holding her close.

This story is about his mother. Most of the stories he makes up are about his mother. About him, about Sunshine, and about his mother.

In this one, they are hiking in the wilderness

when suddenly (things often happen suddenly in his stories) out of nowhere (things often appear out of nowhere, too) a bear leaps out from behind a huge gray boulder.

The bear gnashes its teeth and charges straight at his mother.

She's not going to get hurt, though. His mother never gets hurt in his stories. Sunshine will bark and bark and chase the bear away.

Ben will chase the bear, too. Of course. A dog as small as Sunshine can't chase a bear all by herself.

The story will end when his mom picks Sunshine up and kisses her wet black nose.

Maybe she'll kiss him, too.

He hasn't decided on that part yet.

But the bear . . . he'll help chase the bear for sure. He's never a what-if kid in his stories.

When he and his mother are alone on her island—just the two of them and Sunshine—he'll have lots of time to tell her his new story about the bear. About how Sunshine chased it away. About how he chased the bear, too.

Ben drops another French fry on the floor. It lands next to the first, pale and limp, but Sunshine, lying with her chin on her paws, doesn't even glance at it. He likes to feed her leftovers, but she's not much for eating them.

He slumps in his seat.

Do grown-ups have any idea how boring they can be?

His duffle lies on the bench between him and his dad, and he reaches into it for his tablet. Dad doesn't let him play games at the table when they're eating, but everybody has finished eating. Besides, nobody's paying the least bit of attention to him.

He and his best friend, Russell, are building a dragon, and their dragon needs fire. He'll just check to see if Russell has enough points yet to get fire for their dragon.

His father frowns when he notices the tablet. "I didn't know you brought that," he says. "Not much Wi-Fi up here."

"Wi-Fi!" his mother says. "There's not even electricity on my island."

No electricity! How can anybody live without electricity?

Before Ben can ask, his father's frown shifts from the tablet to Ben's mother. "I didn't realize," he says, "that your cabin would be so . . ." He searches for the word. "Primitive," he says at last.

Something fierce sparks in Ben's mother's eyes. "My cabin has everything we'll need," she says. "Sturdy walls. A wood cookstove. Water from a well. An outhouse."

Ben sits up straighter. *An outhouse!* He has seen only one outhouse in his life. He opened the door, smelled the stink, and decided he didn't really have to go. But he can't do that for a whole week.

His mother looks across the table, not at his dad, at him. "It will be like camping," she says, "except we'll be inside a nice, sturdy cabin."

That doesn't sound so bad. He likes the idea of camping inside a cabin. Once he and Russell tried sleeping in a tent in Russell's backyard, but they had to go inside during the night because it rained right through the tent.

Dad isn't done, though. "If you have no electricity," he says, "then you must not have a phone. I thought for sure you'd have a phone."

"No. No phone. No reception on my island." She says it lightly, but the spark in her eyes is still there.

Ben looks from one parent to the other.

Dad runs his fingers through his hair, pushing it into dark spikes. Ben recognizes those spikes. That's the way his father looks when he's trying to make up his mind. But what is there to make up his mind about? Everything has been decided.

"What if something goes wrong?" Dad asks.

His mother's chin goes high. "What could go wrong? But if something did, we'd paddle back here to town. There are phones here, you know. This is where I come to make calls."

"How long would that take, paddling back here?"

She shrugs. "Two hours. Maybe more if the wind's against us?" It comes out sounding like a question. "There's a bit of portaging, too."

His parents study one another across the table. His father's face is saying "what if" as emphatically as Ben has ever said it. His mother's face says . . . nothing. Nothing at all.

It's clear, though, that she doesn't like what ifs.

After a while, she shrugs again. A whole world of defeat in that shrug. "It's up to you," she says, still speaking to his father. "If you don't want him to come—"

"No!" Ben cries. "Dad, you promised! You said I could go and I'm going!"

His father turns to look at him. He seems startled . . . as though he'd forgotten Ben is still sitting here. His mother looks at him, too. Her eyes are filled with the same flecks of gold light as her hair.

No one speaks.

Finally, his mother reaches a hand across the table toward his father, not far enough to touch, but almost.

"Everything will be all right, David," she says. "No emergencies. I promise."

Ben's father's face says what everyone knows. Emergencies can't be promised away.

But his mother's hand still lies on the table between them, resting there like a small, curled animal. Dad looks at it as if he might gather it up and clasp it to his heart. He doesn't, though.

Instead, he stands abruptly.

Ben knows what that means, too, the way he knows the spiky hair. His mind is made up.

"How many emergencies have you had, living on that island?"

"Not one," she replies, her voice firm. "Not when I was a child and lived there with my grandfather in the summers. Not in these recent years, either."

Dad sighs. He looks down at the hand still resting there, then at Ben's mother. "Okay," he says. "It's okay. I don't suppose emergencies are going to start happening now, just because Ben is visiting."

Ben slumps with relief.

"But . . ." his dad says.

"Please!" he says.

Ben's mother waits.

Ben waits.

"Keep our son safe."

"I will," she says. "I promise." Her voice is strong and very, very certain.

For a long moment his father says nothing more, just stands, studying them both. Finally he adds, "And yourself, too, Lindsey. Keep both of you safe."

She nods, this time quick, almost shy.

Then his parents look at one another, the look long and steady and filled with something very much like love.

Yes! Ben says silently.

He gives Sunshine a nudge with his toe so she can see, too.

Yes!

Now he knows for certain.

His plan is going to work.

Chapter 3
The Beginning of Everything

Two backpacks stuffed with groceries purchased at the general store are settled in the middle of the canoe. Ben's duffle, too. Dad stands on the dock holding the useless tablet he'll be taking home with him.

Ben's mother nods to him. "Step in," she says, pointing to the seat in the front.

Ben steps down into the canoe. It bobbles under his weight. He grabs the sides and sits quickly.

Dad looks down from the dock, his forehead creased. Is he still worrying about no telephone?

His mother gives a quick little jerk of her

chin—a kind of goodbye—and drops lightly into the stern. She's already explained that's what the back of a boat is called, the stern. Even a boat that's only a canoe. The front is the bow.

As she reaches for one of the ropes that hold them to the dock, Ben remembers. *Sunshine! Where is she? Didn't she follow when they left the café?*

He lurches to his feet to scan the dock.

The canoe tips wildly to one side, rights itself, and rolls back the other way.

"Sit down!" The voice behind him is sharp, final.

He sits.

More softly, his mother adds, "Why did you do that, Ben? You could have capsized us."

Ben looks down at the dark water lapping against the canoe. He can swim, and he's wearing a life jacket, so he would have been all right. But what if he had dumped the canoe? The groceries, his duffle. All would be lost.

And he and his mother . . .

For the space of a heartbeat, he imagines the canoe filling with water, both of them surprised, flailing. He pushes the thought away.

"I'm sorry," he says. "I thought I forgot something." And even as he says it, he sees. Why did he think he needed to go looking for Sunshine anyway? She's there. Just the way she always is. Right in front of him, busily raking the aluminum floor to try to fluff it into a bed.

When Sunshine finishes the useless scratching, she curls into a circle and rests her chin on her plumed tail. Her eyes seek out his face.

I'm ready! those eyes say. *Are you ready, too?*

Ready, he answers in that silent way they communicate with one another.

His dad lifts the second rope off the pilings and tosses it into the canoe.

"Goodbye, Benny," he calls. "I'll see you in a week."

There it is again. Benny. As though being with his mother makes him a baby again.

He should hate it, but it's hard to hate anything today. He has everything he wants. He has his mother. For a whole week.

Just about anything can happen in a week.

He takes hold of the wooden paddle lying beneath his seat and pokes it into the water. It feels awkward in his hands, the water unyielding.

His mother pushes off from the dock and they are on their way.

Ben doesn't look back.

So silent.

So slow.

So close to the gleaming water.

The only sound, the faint barks of a V of Canada geese imprinted against the sky, the rhythmic swoosh of paddles.

It takes only a couple dozen strokes for Ben's arms to begin to ache, but he keeps paddling. Or at least he paddles until the ache grows too deep to resist. Then, aware of his mother behind him seeing everything he does, he rests the paddle across his lap. Just for a minute. He's not really stopping.

"Reach forward," she tells him. "Pull the canoe to your paddle. That will help."

Strangely, it does.

Still, the lake ahead seems endless. How long

did she say the paddling would take? Two hours? More?

He wants to talk. He wants to say all sorts of things. But somehow—he doesn't know why—he still can't figure out where to begin. In the stories he makes up, he always knows what to say.

His mother doesn't say much either, except from time to time to give this strange world names. She points out cattails, clumped along the shore. Red-winged blackbirds, swaying on the stems. A short-legged green heron with a fish curved in its beak. A bald eagle floating above them like a bird-shaped kite.

A fish leaps out of the water, belly gleaming gold in the sun. "That's a carp," she tells him, though he wonders how she can tell. It looks like every other fish to him.

When there is nothing more to name, only water and sky, more water and more sky, she falls silent, too.

He considers telling her his latest story, the one about the bear. But now he's not so sure about stories. Maybe stories, like his what-ifs, like the way he depends on Sunshine, are for littler kids.

So he paddles in silence, thinking about the week ahead. A whole week.

When at last they approach the opposite shore, his mother lets the canoe coast to a stop. Then she steps out into the water and gathers the two packs filled with groceries.

"Bring your duffle," she tells him.

Ben rolls his jeans and steps out, too. Cold water fills his sneakers. Slimy lake weed grabs an ankle. He pretends he doesn't mind cold and slimy, just carries his duffle to shore.

When they return for the canoe, Sunshine rides to land perched in the bow like a ship's figurehead.

Canoe and dog safely on the shore, his mother humps one pack onto her back and pulls the second onto her front. She looks like the filling for a pack sandwich.

"This is where we portage to the next lake," she says. "You can manage your duffle, can't you?"

But she doesn't wait for an answer, just begins walking. "It's not far." She tosses the words over her shoulder. "Not even a mile."

Not even a mile!

Ben grabs his duffle, but he's gone only a few steps before he's sorry he let his dad pack for him. There's too much stuff in here.

His mother walks the path that is almost not a path easily, swiftly. As though the packs with all those heavy groceries are filled with feathers. Ben lumbers after.

He spots a boulder up ahead—big enough to hide a bear—but he makes himself look the other way when he passes it. He's not playing at what-ifs anymore. He's giving up on stories, too. Real life is enough.

Hard enough, too.

He looks back from time to time to make sure Sunshine is following.

She is. Sunshine always stays close.

"Are there houses here?" he calls to his mother. "People?"

"There are houses and resorts around the lake we just left," she says. "Very few on the next one where my island is. When you run out of roads, mostly you run out of people."

Except for his mother.

Their destination turns out to be a lake even larger than the one they've just paddled. They deposit backpacks and duffle on the shore then retrace their steps. Ben is glad Sunshine doesn't wander. The trees crowding in on every side look like they could swallow a small dog whole. Maybe a not-so-small boy, too.

When they get back to where they started, his mother hands him the paddles, then flips the canoe onto her shoulders. She doesn't even stagger when it lands, just adjusts her feet to get her balance and strides off, straight and strong.

A paddle over each shoulder, Ben trots to keep up with her. Sunshine trots, too.

We'll be at the cabin soon, he tells himself. *And my arms haven't fallen off yet.*

Today is the beginning of everything. Everything he has ever wanted.

CHAPTER 4
Nothing

The island! They've reached his mother's island! At last!

Ben's arms ache right down to the bones. He'd be happy never to paddle again as long as he lives. But he gives his mother a thumbs-up, climbs out, wades to shore with his duffle, wades back to help carry the canoe onto the shore.

He has the routine down now.

Sunshine has it down, too. She rides to dry land the way she has ridden across the last lake, both paws over the edge of the bow, gazing out over her world as though she owns it. You'd think she'd been a sea dog all her life. A lake dog.

"This way," his mother says, and sandwiched again between the backpacks, she heads up a barely visible path. Ben follows with his duffle, Sunshine trotting behind.

When they step into the wide clearing surrounding the cabin, Ben stops to stare. The cabin is made of logs. It looks like a cabin the early settlers might have built.

"Did you build this?" he asks.

If his mother can flip a canoe, carry it on her shoulders, paddle forever without stopping, she must be able to do anything.

But she shakes her head. "I inherited it from my grandfather."

Ben takes that in. He's never met her grandfather. He's never met anyone in her family. *His* family.

Just the way every kid he knows has a mother, they have two sets of grandparents, too. Except him.

The thought of the "except him" twists in his gut. Just a bit.

"Your grandfather must have really liked you," he says, "to leave you something so . . ." His words trail off. He can't think of any way to describe the cabin.

"So grand?" his mother says. She laughs. But then she adds softly, "He did. He really did."

She stops, starts again. "When I was a kid, I spent every summer up here with Gramps. They were the happiest times of my life. They were pretty much the only happy times. That's why—"

But once again she stops, and this time she doesn't start up again. Having reached the door, she just opens it and steps inside.

Why what? Ben wonders. *Why she came here? To be happy?*

Wasn't she happy at home with him and his dad?

He follows her into dark as deep as a bear's cave. The walls are thick, the thickness of the old trees the cabin is built from. The windows are small and high and set so deep that little light filters through.

Ben drops his duffle and stands waiting, though he's not sure what he's waiting for. To be invited into his mother's life?

She crosses the room, slips off the packs, and lays them on a table. It must be a table, but Ben can barely make it out.

A scritching sound. The tang of a struck match. Flame blooms in a lantern.

Ben moves through the new softer darkness toward the glowing lantern.

The table is made out of logs, too, except these logs are flattened on one side and the surface has been polished until it gleams. In addition to the lantern and now the packs that his mother has just put there, the table is littered with paper, pens, books, dishes left over from this morning's breakfast. Probably from last night's supper as well. A crumpled sweatshirt lies at one end, empty arms hanging over the edge as though it has given up.

His father would hate this table. Not the fact that it's made out of logs. The clutter.

Everything around his father must be neat. If it isn't, he'll get it that way in short order. Every Saturday he cleans the house, top to bottom, bottom to top. And the kitchen, the kitchen he cleans every single day. Ben was still so small that he had to step up on a stool to reach the sink when he learned to rinse his dishes and put them into the dishwasher as soon as he finished a meal.

His mother's cabin is messy, just plain messy, but it looks . . . nice.

"This is great," he says, turning slowly to take it all in. "Your cabin is really great." The whole cabin is no bigger than their living room at home. Maybe not as big.

An iron cooking stove stands along one wall. Pots and pans are jumbled on the surface. There is a strange sink with no faucets, too.

A crumpled sleeping bag on a low platform seems to be his mother's bed.

A rickety dresser, drawers half open. Underwear hangs out of one of the drawers. Ben can feel himself flush when he catches sight of it.

He looks away.

More shelves next to the bed. Books and notebooks. Lots of books and notebooks.

The only other furniture is a rocker. No other

chairs in the room. Does his mother never have visitors? Didn't she expect to have him visit someday?

There is no second bed. Not even a futon that could serve as a bed.

"Where will I sleep?" he asks.

"In the loft." She points high and toward one end of the cabin.

In the gloom he can just make out the loft. Very high up. His heart pounds. He's hated heights since the time he and his friend Toby climbed the enormous oak in Toby's backyard. They climbed the tree together, and Toby climbed down alone.

Ben didn't get scared until he looked down, but once he did, it wasn't his usual what-if flashing through his brain. It was just a flat "I'm going to fall! I know it!" He wrapped his arms around the trunk and refused to move another inch.

He didn't so much refuse to move. He simply couldn't. If a cougar had appeared on the limb he was sitting on, he couldn't have let go to climb down.

Sometimes Toby still teases about his dad having to climb up and half carry Ben out of the oak.

Ben has never climbed that tree—or any other—since. And the slender ladder leaning against the loft looks a lot less sturdy than Toby's tree.

"I can't sleep up there," he says.

A single eyebrow goes up. The eyebrow is ginger like his mother's hair, and it looks almost too vivid against her pale skin. *Why not?* the raised eyebrow asks.

"Because . . ." he says. He stops. He looks down at Sunshine as though she's going to come up with an answer.

She has followed him in, of course, but now she is lying stretched out on the floor, halfway between him and his mother.

What can he say? Because my dog doesn't know how to climb ladders?

His mother waits. Not an impatient kind of waiting. She looks set to wait for a long time. But it's the kind of waiting that expects an answer.

"Because . . ." he says again, then he finishes

with the only thing he can think of. The truth. "I don't like high places. I got stuck in a tree once."

"I didn't know that," his mother says. She stands there considering him as though he's a problem to be solved, which isn't what he wants at all.

At last she says, "You could sleep on the floor. Down here next to me."

He likes the idea of "down here next to me." It must be dark up in that loft, too. And that is something else she doesn't know about him. He hates the dark. Still, he gives himself a mental shake and says, "Never mind. I'll be fine. The loft looks neat."

And to prove it, he slips the strap of the duffle over one shoulder and climbs rapidly, taking care not to look down. He pretends not to notice the way his knees go soft the moment he steps onto the first rung. He pretends the duffle isn't pulling at his shoulder so hard that it nearly unbalances him, too.

When he reaches the top, he hefts his duffle next to another sleeping bag, this one spread on the floor, and backs down the ladder again. He does it all in one swift motion, without giving himself a chance to see or even to think about the empty space yawning below.

He steps down onto the floor and looks to Sunshine for approval. She knows how he hates high-up places. She knows everything about him.

But the trip must have tired her out. She usually watches him every minute. That's her job, watching him. Now she's stretched on the floor, her back legs poking straight out behind, chin resting on her paws, eyes closed. Sound asleep. She didn't even see what he did.

His mother paid no attention, either. She's busy putting away groceries, and now she's coming toward him, a carton of eggs in each hand. She's not paying the least bit of attention to the small dog sprawled directly in her path.

"Stop!" Ben cries. "You're going to step on . . . !"

His mother stops.

She stops and stares.

At him.

Then she looks down at her feet, at the floor in front of her feet, and then at him again. "Ben?" she says. It's a question.

But he can't explain. There's no way. Because Sunshine isn't there. Not really.

She has never been there.

He knows that. Even when he forgets, he knows.

Sunshine is a story, an imaginary dog dreamed up by a three-year-old kid.

A story dog that has hung around far too long. At least that's what his father thinks. And now his mother will think the same.

But she doesn't seem to be thinking anything. She's just standing there waiting for an explanation.

"It's nothing," he says finally. "It's just . . . nothing."

She goes on studying him until he begins to itch. Then, at last, she says, "Okay. Let me show you the neat little cooler I have. It's right here beneath the floor."

And when she lifts a couple of boards to show him the deep hole dug beneath the floor and the bucket on a rope that can be lowered into the earth to keep food cool, Ben pretends to be very interested.

Chapter 5
Wolves

Ben's eyes open slowly. He hurts everywhere. His arms still ache from paddling. His hands. His shoulders. His back. But the sleeping bag is warm, and it smells of earth and pine needles.

He props on one elbow to check for Sunshine. It's the first thing he does every morning, look to see where she is. He knows she's not real. Of course. She just lives in his mind. But still, when he looks he can always find her.

And there she is. Curled on a corner of the sleeping bag below his feet.

Ben pats the floor to call her closer. She opens one eye, considers his invitation, then lets her eye drift closed again.

Ben flops back down, astonished. His dog never disobeys him. Never!

But then, as if to let him know she was only teasing, Sunshine rises, pads toward him, and lies down again with a small grunt, half on, half off his pillow. She gives his ear a good-morning lick.

He sighs and turns toward her until her reddish-gold fur fills his whole vision. There's never been a moment when he couldn't count on her.

When Ben was younger, his dad liked Sunshine, too. He'd ask what she was doing and sometimes even pretend to play with her. It's only lately he's changed his mind. Only lately he's decided Ben is "too old" for an imaginary friend. That's what he calls Sunshine, "your imaginary friend."

Ben squeezes his eyes shut and opens them again. A small test.

She's still here, right next to his face.

He closes his hand around a floppy ear. He can't

count the number of times he's held an ear, warm and furry in his hand. When he was little, he used to hold it all night long while he slept.

It's what drives his dad crazy, the way he "touches" Sunshine. He says it's taking imaginings too far. He also says there are some things a person has to grow out of.

Ben says . . . well, he doesn't say anything, really. But he hasn't given up Sunshine. Hasn't quit "touching" her, either.

Movement below. A pan clanks against the iron stove. That means his mother is up. Fixing breakfast. For him.

She never asked what it was he tried to keep her from stepping on last night. She just waited for him to explain, and when he didn't, she went on showing him around. She showed him the cooler beneath the floor, the outside pump where she got her water to carry into the house, the outhouse.

By the time they sat down to supper, though, she had run out of things to say. And the long list of topics he'd been gathering seemed, once more, to have floated away, so mostly he was quiet, too.

She did ask him what position he likes to play in baseball, and he told her first base. But he also said that his best friend Russell will probably get it. "It's hard to get first base," he explained, "if you miss the first week of practice."

"I'm sorry," she said. As though his missing practice was her fault.

Then because he didn't want her to think he was blaming her, he told her the truth. Russell probably would have gotten first base anyway, because Russell's a lefty, and lefties always have the best shot at first base.

He didn't tell her the other truth, that Russell is a better player than he is.

Sunshine nuzzles Ben's ear. He takes her snub face between his hands and nuzzles her back, nose to nose. She sneezes.

"I'll bet you need to go out, don't you?" he says, though he's the one who needs to go. Sometimes he likes to pretend it's her, though.

He sits up. "Ready?"

Sunshine does a play bow, paws outstretched, rump high, eyes sparkling.

Ben scrambles out of the sleeping bag, pulls on his damp jeans and soggy sneakers. He has dry clothes in his duffle, but he doesn't want to take the time to unpack. "I'll beat you downstairs," he tells her.

He hesitates for a few beats at the edge of the loft, looking everywhere but down. Then he turns around, closes his eyes, feels for the top rung with his toe, and climbs fast. Like it's something he does every day.

Just in case she's watching.

Sunshine doesn't have to worry about the ladder. Once Ben reaches the floor, she's there, too. Right next to him.

His mother is standing at the cookstove stirring something in a pot.

Whatever she's making for breakfast isn't animal-shaped pancakes for sure. Oatmeal, maybe. He hates oatmeal. Dad never makes it because he knows how much Ben hates it.

"Good morning," she says. "Who were you talking to up there?"

A warning ripples the length of his back. He

should have been more careful. He's getting used to being careful around his father.

"Oh," he says, "it's just . . . just . . ." He pulls in a breath and apologizes silently to Sunshine. "Just a game I like to play."

"What kind of game?" she asks, her face open and expectant as though she really wants to know. Her long hair is divided into two braids this morning, wound around her head in a coppery crown. She looks pretty.

Ben takes a step toward the door. Can he pretend he didn't hear?

When he glances back, she's still looking at him.

"Was it the same game you were playing last night?" she asks. "When you stopped me from stepping on something? On somebody?"

The question pins Ben to the spot. He can feel Sunshine pressing against his leg. It's what she does to let him know she's here. But even that doesn't help.

"It's just a story I like to tell myself," he says, speaking fast and low. "About my dog. About my pretend dog." He comes down hard on the word *pretend.* "I . . . I made her up when I was little, and I've kind of gotten used to her. So I've kept her around. In my mind, you know. And sometimes I talk to her . . . just for fun."

He waits for her to say it. He's too old for a pretend dog.

But she just goes on studying him, her head tipped, her eyes bright. And when she speaks at last, it's only to ask, "Male or female?"

"Female," Ben says, surprised, but trying to match her matter-of-fact tone. "Her name is Sunshine."

His mother nods. "Nice name," she says. Then she adds, "Everyone needs a daemon." And she turns back to stir whatever is in the pot.

Ben stands perfectly still. "A demon? Like a devil?"

"No. A daemon . . . like a companion." And she spells it. "D-A-E-M-O-N. A guardian spirit. A daemon usually takes the form of an animal."

She says it casually, as though lots of people go around with guardian spirits.

Ben couldn't be more delighted. That's exactly what Sunshine is, what she has always been.

"Do you have a daemon?" he asks.

"I can't say that I do," she answers. "I wouldn't mind having one, though."

Ben wants to talk more about daemons, but the reason he came down from the loft tugs at him, so he says instead, "Gotta go," and heads out the door.

His daemon follows him into the morning.

Once he's outside, Ben looks down at Sunshine and laughs. "My mother likes you!" he tells her. "She really does!"

Sunshine wags her tail. If Ben had a tail, he'd wag, too.

His mother didn't say a thing about "too old." She even understands what Sunshine means to him. A daemon, a companion, a guardian spirit.

Who would have thought a mother, any mother in the world, could be so perfect? He does a small, delighted dance before he says, "Come on, Sunshine," and heads for the outhouse.

The day is fresh and cool, the sky a startling

blue. The scent of evergreen trees and lake lies on the air.

He approaches the outhouse cautiously. Last night when his mother pointed it out, he didn't go near. Before bed, when she sent him out to use it, he stood gaping at the stars scattered across the sky. He'd never seen so many. The wash of city light in St. Paul chases most of the stars away.

Then he walked to the edge of the clearing that surrounded the cabin and peed on a tree.

He has to do more than pee now, though. Nothing to do but check out the outhouse.

He opens the door cautiously. The hole in the wooden bench reminds him of when he was really little, back when he was convinced a flushing toilet could swallow him whole. No flushing here, but it doesn't take much of an imagination to call up menaces hidden in the smelly dark beneath the hole.

Spiders, toads, snakes.

Alligators.

This is the Northwoods. No alligators. But anything else seems possible. Anything savage.

"Want to come in?" he asks Sunshine, holding the door wide.

She peers into his face, pretending not to understand.

"Have it your way," he tells her, because clearly she intends to. Should his daemon be quite so independent? And he lets the door bang closed behind him.

It isn't until he emerges that he hears it.

A wavering howl. Rising and rising. The kind of sound that stiffens the hair on the back of your neck.

Ben freezes, trying to separate the sound from the mist hanging over the morning lake and lapping the shore.

Nothing lies in the direction of the call, just the edge of the island and the misty lake beyond.

Then an answering wail, this time from behind him on the other side of the island. Or on the lake beyond. He can't tell.

Equally close. Every bit as eerie.

This call, too, rises, wobbles, vibrates.

Mournful.

Plaintive.

Chilling.

He's trapped!

Ben's feet are running before his brain has even found the word. Running and running.

He slams through the cabin door.

"Wolves!" he gasps. "There are wolves out there! They almost got me!"

For an instant his mother stands still, holding high the wooden spoon she's been stirring with as though she's going to use it against the wolves. Then her face softens.

She drops the spoon into the pot and hurries toward him.

"Oh," she cries. "Oh, my dear!" And she wraps her arms around him, pulling him close. "There *are* wolves up here. Of course. But that's not wolves you're hearing. Haven't you heard loons before? They're the state bird, after all."

For an instant Ben dissolves into the comfort, the familiar safety of the hug. *It's loons! Only loons! I know about loons! Though who knew they sounded like that?*

But then she goes and does it. She spoils everything.

She grasps his shoulders, holds him away from
her to look directly into his face, and she laughs.
Not a loud laugh, but a heartfelt one. Thoroughly
amused. Just the way she laughed when he first
greeted her. As though his being scared, his mis-
taking loons for wolves, is the funniest thing ever.

Anger flashes in Ben's gut like a gasoline-fed
fire. His mother, his own mother, is making fun of
him.

He jerks away and heads for the door.

He has to go back to find Sunshine.

CHAPTER 6
The Shrug

Ben stops on the other side of the slammed door and looks around. Sunshine is gone . . . again.

Head down, he scuffs through the fallen evergreen needles that cover the island like a rug. Brown and dry and ugly. Who says the Northwoods are so beautiful? Not a bit of grass around his mother's cabin. Just rocks and dead needles and brush. Weeds, really.

His mother knows the difference between wolves and loons, but she doesn't know weeds from grass. A house is supposed to have grass around it.

And his dog is supposed to stay close. Usually

he has only to think about her for her to be here. Right next to him. Watching over him.

He starts down the path toward the lake.

It's probably his mother's fault that she isn't here. Maybe Sunshine doesn't like being called a "daemon."

"Sunshine!" he calls. "Come on, girl!" And more emphatically, "Sunshine! Come here! Right now!"

No dog.

But when he circles a clump of white-barked birch trees, there she is, sitting next to the overturned canoe. She's so intent on staring off across the water that she doesn't even turn to look at him.

Ben walks up quietly, settles on the rocky ground beside her, and buries his face in his hands.

Loons! It was only loons! How could he have been so dumb? Now his mother knows the worst thing about him, the thing he most didn't want her to know. What a scaredy-cat he is.

Scared of the state bird.

And she doesn't know the half of it.

He's not just scared of birds that sound like wolves and scared of high-up places, the things she's already found out. Sometimes he's even afraid of stuff other kids love, like a baseball hurtling toward him at a hundred miles per hour.

That's why he's not such a great player. He's pretty good at hitting the ball. He even got a home run once. And he's not so bad at throwing. But sometimes when the ball is coming at him fast and hard, something inside him wants to duck. It's not easy to make a good catch when your insides are trying to duck.

She doesn't know that he sleeps with a nightlight on at home, either.

Or that he gets bad dreams from watching TV programs where people get killed.

Or that he has no sense of direction, so he's always afraid of getting lost. Dad teases him, says he can lose his way walking around a city block. And that's almost true.

His father is patient about all his scared. He just says, "It's okay, Ben. Everything's okay." And then, mostly, it is. But there's no way his mother, who lives alone in the wilderness surrounded by wild animals and dark nights, will understand scared.

Ben grinds his fists into his eye sockets. He's got to keep on top of his plan. The whole reason he asked to visit will be ruined if he's not careful.

He's worked everything out. To come here. To spend a whole week here. With his mother. So she'll get to know him again. So she'll get to know what a great kid he has grown to be. So she'll want him.

And if she wants him, she'll decide to come home with him. She'll decide to come home and stay. For sure.

Won't she?

Dad wants her to come home, too. He hasn't said so, but Ben is sure he does.

He shaved just to see her, didn't he?

It doesn't matter that they're divorced, that they got divorced a long time ago. Because there's no rule that says divorced people can't get married again . . . to one another. That's what happened to a girl in his class. Her parents were divorced when she was little, then they married again last year.

Which is what got him to thinking about his mother, about how he could get her to come home.

And even though she laughed at him—and it's really rude to laugh at somebody who's just scared—that's what he wants. Still.

If only he hadn't started out so wrong.

He lays a hand on Sunshine's back and takes a deep breath.

He hasn't really done anything so terrible yet. Only mistaken loons for wolves. And he paddled all the way here, didn't he? Without once saying his arms were tired. He didn't say anything about sleeping in the dark, either. He admitted he didn't like high-up places, but then he turned around and climbed up to the loft. So that showed her he's pretty brave.

And his mother seems almost to like Sunshine. To like the idea of her, anyway. And what else is Sunshine but an idea?

It isn't enough, though, for her to like his dog. By the end of the week, she's got to like *him*.

"Come on," he says to Sunshine. "Let's go back in and pretend oatmeal is the best breakfast in the world."

The oatmeal isn't bad. Really. His mother stirred raisins and walnuts into it, then she put a big pat of butter to melt on the top of his serving and poured maple syrup over that.

"Dad's oatmeal isn't half as good as this," Ben says around a mouthful of buttery sweetness. He doesn't look at her when he says it, though. He's still pretty embarrassed about running in here, scared to death of loons.

"I'm glad you like it," she answers. "Your dad's a better cook than I am, though. He's better at lots of things."

"Like what?" Ben asks, startled into meeting her gaze. Dad is great. Really. And he cooks just fine. But his food—everything about him—comes with so many rules. He would never top oatmeal with butter and syrup. *Too much fat! Too much sugar!* That's what he would say.

Dad couldn't live in a log cabin without electricity or a phone, either. He likes everything just so, and there's not much "just so" here.

His mother shrugs. "For one thing, he's a better teacher than I am. I was teaching English at his high school when we met. Now he's still teaching, and I . . ."

She stops and starts again.

"You did everybody a favor by being born, Ben. Your dad and me, of course. But you did the school a favor, too. If I'd been teaching chemistry like your dad, the school would have probably gotten blown up. I didn't exactly have control of my class."

Ben can hardly believe it. She didn't have control of her class? Wouldn't those kids know just from looking at her that this woman can flip a canoe and carry it on her shoulders?

"Did you *like* teaching English?" he asks.

Again that shrug. "I liked what I taught," she says. "But I didn't much like teaching. The students seemed to feel obligated to hate everything they read just because it was assigned. And the whole point of teaching literature, it seems to me, is to teach people to love to read, to want to do it all their lives. If they're going to hate everything before they look at it . . . well, what's the point?"

Ben wants to defend the kids, but he doesn't

know how. Then he wants to defend his mother, too, and he doesn't know how to do that, either.

She rescues him by changing the subject. "Did you know you're not the first one to mistake the call of loons for howling wolves? The early settlers did that, too. When they first heard loons, they were really scared."

Warmth flows through Ben's body. A happy flush that sets him tingling right down to his toes. Maybe he didn't mess up as badly as he thought.

He takes another bite of oatmeal. It's about as good as it's possible for oatmeal to be.

His mother is as good as it's possible for a mother to be, too.

"Did the loons ever scare you?" he asks.

"Maybe when I was a little girl. Back when I first started to come up here with my gramps. But I learned to love their call. You will, too, Ben. It's eerie, but it's strangely beautiful."

So even his mother, his fierce, strong mother, might have been afraid of loons once. Ben relaxes a bit more. He tries to think of something else to say to keep the conversation going.

"You were happy here with your . . . gramps? Weren't you happy at home?"

A shadow passes across his mother's face. "My mother was never happy with me. I wasn't what she wanted. I'm not sure what she wanted, but it wasn't me."

"How did you know?" Ben asks softly.

A guffaw, short and sharp. Not a happy sound. "Well, for one thing, she hit me just about every time I turned around. When I was little, I just figured that was the way the world was made. You do something, you don't know what, and you get hit. Or maybe you don't do something, and you get hit for not doing it. Then she would love me up. Then she would explode and hit me again. I never knew which end was up."

Ben lets his mother's words settle. He's sorry for the little girl his mother was. Really, truly sorry. But another question pushes past all that sorry, and he has to ask it. "Did you like me?" he says. "Was *I* what *you* wanted?" Something deep inside him trembles as he says it.

"You?" That laugh again. "Who wouldn't want

you? You were the kind of kid any mother would want."

The words fill Ben to the brim, but as fast as they do, they run out of him again, leaving him emptier than before.

But did you *want me?* his heart cries. *Not any mother. You.*

That seems too hard to say, though. He goes back to applying himself to his oatmeal. He's not sure he wants to hear the answer anyway.

For a few moments there is no sound in the room except spoons clinking against bowls, then his mother says, almost casually, "Your dad. He's good to you, isn't he?"

The question comes with a bright, inquisitive smile, and something that is almost anger rises inside Ben.

Good to him! Of course, his dad is good to him. The way every parent he knows is "good" to their kids.

He's there. Every day and every night, he's there. He makes the meals and buys the stuff Ben needs and some stuff he doesn't need, too. And he always checks to make sure homework is done. He listens when Ben's worried about something. And Dad worries, too. About him. Worries too much sometimes. And sometimes he's a bit too particular.

But *good* to him? Of course!

If she thinks he doesn't need *her* just because his dad is good to him! Well . . .

"Yeah," he says. "Dad's good to me." But even as he says it, the anger that rushed through him seeps away. That's the way it always is. He gets angry sometimes just thinking about his mother, but he's like a balloon that can't hold air. Almost before he knows what's happening, he goes limp and flat again.

"I knew he would be," his mother says. And she sounds satisfied, like something is settled. Like his dad's being good to him makes everything all right.

Another bump of anger, but this time Ben pushes it away.

He is scraping the bottom of his bowl when his mother asks, "Are you ready for an adventure?"

She's smiling, and Ben smiles back. "Sure," he says.

Wisps of mist leap away from the bow of the canoe like startled ghosts.

Ben likes pretending the mist is ghosts. Ghosts that don't scare him one little bit.

He and his mother paddle around to the other side of the island, then across to the mainland shore and into a deep lagoon. They pull up so close to the base of a waterfall that he could wash his face in the spray.

If he wanted to wash his face.

An enormously tall blue-gray bird stands at the edge of the water, just out of reach of the spray.

"That's a great blue heron," his mother tells him.

The bird hesitates for a few beats, studying them with a golden eye, then stretches its wings out and out and out and floats away, its long legs trailing after. It scolds as it flies, craggy and hoarse.

"They're very shy," his mother says. "So many were killed off back when their beautiful feathers were wanted for ladies' hats. Only the timid survived, and timid birds make timid babies."

She gives Ben that nod he is beginning to recognize, one that means she's just made a point.

"That," she says, "is the way survival of the fittest works. In this case, to survive you had to be timid enough to keep out of sight."

Ben likes that idea. If he were a great blue heron, it would be useful to be a scaredy-cat. A scaredy-bird!

They see ravens, too, a huge flock of the big black birds. Bigger than the crows at home with larger, more curved beaks.

"Some folks say ravens help the wolves hunt," his mother says. "They say they lead them to game so they can share the spoils."

Ben takes it all in.

When a doe comes to the water to drink, followed by two dappled, spindle-legged fawns, he holds his breath.

The babies sniff the water, dip their noses, come up snorting.

Demonstrating how it's done, the mama laps

water gracefully. The fawns give up, though, and gambol away. Mama follows, the white flags of their tails waving goodbye.

Sunshine watches all this from her perch in the bow, her head raised, her long ears slightly cupped to catch every sound.

Each time something new comes into view, Ben looks back to check his mother's face. She must have seen such sights a thousand times, but she looks as entranced as he is.

What will it be like for her to be back in the city?

Never mind. She'll still have her cabin. The two of them can come back here in the summer. Sunshine, too. Maybe even his dad will want to come. He smiles at the thought of his dad in the messy cabin, his dad without electricity and phone, his dad using a stinky outhouse. They paddle out of the lagoon and along a rocky beach.

"Let's go ashore," his mother says after a time, and they do, pulling up close, then climbing out and lifting the canoe between them to carry it to land.

"Come," she says. Just that. *Come.* And he follows.

They walk along the shore a ways, Sunshine tagging after. When his mother steps off the pebbled beach and into the woods, Ben and Sunshine both stay close behind. He can see no trail that she's following, but she moves quickly and without swerving as though she is on one.

The lush undergrowth grabs at his feet, and an occasional rotting log lies in their path. His mother just steps through and over whatever is in their path, pushing her way through the branches of the towering evergreens. He does, too.

Just when he is ready to call out, to ask where they are going, she comes to an abrupt halt in front of him. He steps up beside her. Sunshine settles at his feet.

They are standing at the edge of a clearing filled with cheerful yellow flowers. The woods they have been walking through are dappled and dark, but the sudden break in the trees lets the sunlight through. The yellow blooms glow as though the light radiates up from the earth.

Ben looks around. He can't help but be disappointed. Just flowers?

They are pretty, though. Beautiful, even.

His mother stands perfectly still, saying nothing, so he says nothing, too.

"Marsh marigolds," she says finally, speaking in a low voice as though the flowers might hear and flee. "This is one of my favorite spots this time of year."

He nods. He doesn't know why exactly, but he's glad she has favorite spots, places that make her feel at home.

Though he wishes she would feel at home in St. Paul.

With his dad.

With him.

Ben studies the bright, expectant yellow, waiting for his mother's signal to turn back. He's seen the flowers. The flowers and the trees, the trees, the trees. He shifts his weight, the readiness to move on filling his body.

Then he takes a deep breath. Where does he want to be off to anyway? He's here. Next to this mother. Isn't this what he's dreamed a thousand times? A hundred thousand?

He hasn't been this close to her since he got here. Always a table between them. Or the length of a canoe. Except when he came running in, scared by the loons' weird, warbling call. She hugged him then.

Hugged him before she spoiled it all by laughing.

Last night when it was time for bed, she offered no hug. He even dawdled a while to see if she would before he climbed to the loft.

Dad always hugs him at bedtime. Even if Ben has a friend staying over, Dad insists on a hug. And Ben's not supposed to mind.

He doesn't really, but . . .

"I saw a moose here once," his mother says. She speaks in a hushed voice the way people do in church. "Only once. We're not apt to see one again. They're dying off or moving north because of the warming climate."

As she speaks, her arm comes up to circle his back. Her hand rests on his shoulder.

The weight of that hand, the warmth of it seeps into Ben's body. He can feel his muscles beneath it go soft.

But then, unbidden, all the years of no warm hand, of no mother come flooding back, and . . . he doesn't decide to do it. Something decides for him. The shoulder beneath the warm hand shrugs.

A small movement, up . . . down.

A tiny pulling away.

It doesn't matter, though, how small the movement is, his mother feels it. She removes her hand.

They don't talk after that. They just walk back to the canoe and start paddling again.

CHAPTER 7
Exploring

Ben doesn't know why it happened. He never told his shoulder to shrug off his mother's hand. It just did it on its own.

He wants to say something. *I'm sorry. I didn't mean it. I didn't mean it at all.*

But that shrug was such a small thing. Maybe she didn't notice.

Except she *did* notice. He knows she did. Why else did she take her hand away? Why did she go so quiet?

Practically his whole life he's wanted his mother,

wanted her close and close and close, and then when he finally has her, what does he do?

Shrugs her away, that's what.

Emptiness gripped his shoulder the instant her hand lifted away. Gripped it all the way back to the cabin. Grips it still as he sits at the gleaming log table waiting for lunch.

She sets a sandwich in front of him, and he studies it. It's easier to look at the sandwich than at her. He lifts the top slice. Two slices of ham. Two slices of cheese. Nothing else.

Dad would have added mayo and mustard. Probably pickle relish, too. Dad loves pickle relish. He loves pickle relish so much he forgets Ben doesn't like pickles.

His mother sits down across from him, ham and cheese rolled into a tube in her hand. No mayo or mustard on hers, either. Not even any bread.

Sunshine, his usually loyal Sunshine, has stayed close to his mother's side while she fixed the food. Now she settles at her feet.

"I'd love to hear more about your dog," his mother says, breaking the silence at last.

"Like what?" Does she know Sunshine is following her around? Is that why she's asking?

"Oh, I don't know. Like tell me what she's doing."

Ben looks down at his feet, at the emptiness there. "Right now?" he asks.

She nods.

"She's sitting by my feet. She's leaning against my leg. It's what she always does. To let me know she's there."

His mother nods again, believing every word. So she *can't* see his dog. And then she proves it by asking "What does she look like?"

He tells her—the snub nose, the long ears, the soft, slightly curly coat. The plumed tail.

"Is she with you all the time? Does she go with you to school? And to your friends' houses?"

"Sure," he says. He takes a bite of the dry sandwich, chews, sets it back on the plate. When the silence that follows his abrupt answer grows uncomfortable, even for him, he adds, "At recess she likes to chase me when I run."

His mother chuckles, enjoying the idea of Sunshine chasing him on the playground.

"Has anyone else seen her? Your dad? Any of your friends?"

Ben considers that. Not his dad for sure. Russell used to say he saw Sunshine when they were both little. But that was just pretend. A different pretend than his.

Can you pretend to pretend?

Russell used to say Sunshine was doing stuff she would never really do, undoglike stuff. Standing on her head or snuggling in Russell's lap. Ben was kind of relieved when Russell quit "seeing" Sunshine.

"She's *my* dog," he says. "She doesn't show herself to just anybody."

His mother nods as though that's a perfectly reasonable answer.

He picks up the sandwich, studies it, sets it down again. "Don't you have any mayo?" he asks. "Or mustard?"

"Sorry," she says. "No room in my cooler for things like that."

"Pickle relish?" he adds.

Now why did he say that?

His mother looks surprised. "You've changed," she says. "You used to hate pickles. Dill or sweet, you'd have nothing to do with them."

"Yeah," Ben says. "I've changed."

He reaches to the empty floor next to his foot and pretends to scratch Sunshine behind her left ear.

How she loves—used to love—being scratched behind her left ear.

His mother picks up his plate with his barely touched sandwich. "How about I toast this in a pan with some butter," she says. "Then it won't be so dry."

It's okay, Ben wants to say. *I like it just the way it is.*

But he lets her take the dry sandwich away. Which leaves him with more to make up for—not just the shoulder shrug, but not liking the way she makes sandwiches, too.

His mother stirs the coals in the cooking stove, adds kindling to build up the fire, picks a frying pan off the floor and puts it on the stove. When she returns the sandwich, it is golden and crunchy on the outside, warm and melty inside.

Then she sits down across from him again. All is quiet except for the sounds inside his own head, the sounds of chewing, of swallowing.

"Ben," she says.

He looks up, but she says nothing more. He waits.

"Ben," she says again, "I know you're angry, but—"

"I'M NOT ANGRY!" The words come out louder than he had intended. Bigger and taller, too.

His mother's eyebrows go up like twin flags.

"I'm not angry," he says again, more quietly this time.

She studies him. He can feel the heat flaming in his cheeks. Even his ears burn.

"There's nothing wrong with being angry, you know?" she says after a time. "It's just a feeling. It doesn't hurt anybody. Besides, you have good reason."

"But I'm *not*." Ben insists. "I'm really, truly not!"

It's that stupid shrug, he knows. Has he spoiled his whole plan with a shrug?

"Okay," his mother says. Just that. *Okay*. Then she falls silent again.

Dad would argue with him. He would go on and on about how it's good to talk about feelings until Ben would want to scream, but his mother just says *okay*, and she's done.

He likes that about her.

He takes big bites of the sandwich, chews as fast as he can, a new plan forming. He knows how he can show her how not-angry he is!

"How about Sunshine and I go outside now?" he says after he's swallowed the last bite and is brushing the buttery crumbs from his hands. "We'll stay for the whole afternoon. Then you'll have time to work on your novel. Just like you would if you didn't have me here."

His mother looks startled. "Are you sure?" she asks, but even as she says it, a light turns on behind her eyes. He's hit the jackpot. He couldn't have come up with a better idea.

"I'm sure," he says.

And he is.

"The two of you can explore," she says, clearly enthusiastic. More enthusiastic than she needs to be. "There's lots to discover on my island."

"Of course," Ben says. "We'll explore." He even chuckles a bit to show her how much they will enjoy exploring.

He goes to the door and turns back to check on Sunshine. He's not going to call her. He's never had to call her before. She's always stayed with him. But to his great relief, she leaves her place at his mother's feet and comes. Apparently she's decided she's his dog again.

Together they step into the leafy sunshine.

Ben hasn't been traipsing through the brush more than five minutes before he stops to peer back through the trees. Already his mother's cabin has slipped from view.

"What do you think?" he says to Sunshine. "Is this far enough?"

She looks up at him, tail wagging. *Whatever you want,* that wagging tail says. Which is no help at all.

Surely it is far enough. But what do they do now? They can't go back. He promised his mother the whole afternoon for her novel.

What's it like to work on a novel anyway? Different probably than letting a story gather in your mind as you stare out the window of a car.

Different and maybe a little bit the same, too.

Off to one side a fallen tree offers itself as a bench. If they stay here, he won't have to worry about getting lost. And his mother won't know they're not really exploring.

He sits on the tree-bench, and Sunshine, back to doing her job, lies at his feet. She gazes up at him as though he's the most important person in the world.

Not much point in more exploring anyway. Everything on this island looks the same. Green and growing or gray and rocky. He'll just wait here for the afternoon to pass, and then he'll go back.

The quiet is strange and deep. The only sound, a cascading stream of notes from inside a nearby pine. The invisible bird sounds happy. Almost as happy as *he* should be. Being here. With his mother.

At last.

It's not that he's *not* happy. It's just that . . . He doesn't know how to name what it is. Except that he's trying so hard. Every minute, trying.

When he's with his dad, he just . . . is.

He's not angry, though. Like she said. She's got that wrong.

The birdsong stops and a chittering chipmunk takes over. The noisy thing scurries along the fallen tree trunk, sees Ben, probably sees Sunshine, too, changes its little mind, and scurries back, tail pumping. You'd think it's the pumping tail that generates all that hurry.

They have birds and chipmunks in St. Paul. Squirrels and rabbits, too. Even wild turkeys and deer. One night a deer came and nibbled the blooms off every one of Dad's brand-new iris right out of their front yard.

Up here they have all those and other creatures, too. Bears. Wolves!

He's not going to think about wolves. The
afternoon will be long enough without thinking
about wolves.

Does his father know there are wolves up here?
Would he have let him come if he did?

Thinking about his father makes Ben wonder.
What is Dad doing now?

Not starting the patio yet, Ben hopes, the one
Dad's planning to build on the back of the house
this summer. He promised Ben he could help. Russell, too.

And Russell. What about him? Has he found
fire for their dragon yet? It would be easier to sit
out here for the whole, long afternoon if he had
his tablet.

The truth is, he never wanted a week on an
island. Not really. What he wanted—what he
wants still—is to get to the end of the week, to
arrive at the moment when he can ask the question he came here to ask.

When his mother says yes, when she comes home with him, he'll be like other kids, other kids who have mothers. Some kids he knows don't have dads, not dads who live with them anyway. But everybody has a mother.

Always, always he's wanted one, too.

Ben has tried from time to time to get his father to date, to go out and find him a new mother. He never did. So Ben decided this mother, the mother he could barely remember before he got here, had to be the one to be found.

Which was where his plan began.

When his mother comes home with them, everything will be different. Easier. Even talking will be easier then. It won't be just the two of them and all this nothing the way it is now. They can watch TV together, and they can talk about the program. She can go to his baseball games, and they can talk about how well he played.

And she and his dad can talk and talk the way parents do. Stuff he doesn't even have to listen to. Because their talking will mean that they are together, all three of them together. And it will mean that he's just another kid. Like everybody else.

This is the way the afternoon goes. Ben sits until his butt grows flat from sitting. His mind skitters from one topic to the next, but keeps coming back to his mother. Over and over again, his mother. Then, when the sun finally begins to drop down the other side of the sky, he stands, stretches, and heads back to the cabin. He feels very grown-up. As though he's somebody who's really been exploring.

His mother will see she'll still have plenty of time to work on her novel when she comes home. She'll see how considerate he is. How easy to have around.

The kind of kid any mother would want.

CHAPTER 8
Something Special

A perfect morning! Pancakes for breakfast! And not just ordinary pancakes, either. Ben's mother makes the animal shapes he remembered better than he remembered her face.

And so much crisp bacon that he couldn't eat all she piled on his plate. Dad always makes exactly two slices each.

Now here they are in the canoe again, off on another adventure.

Could anything be better?

"I can't predict what we'll see," his mother says, her voice drifting to him from the stern. "It's different every time I go. But I'm hoping for something special."

What kind of something? Ben wonders. *What kind of special?* But he doesn't ask. He loves surprises.

At least he thinks he loves surprises.

Sunshine rides in her usual place in the bow, and the paddle feels familiar, almost comfortable, in Ben's hands.

Maybe this afternoon when he's on his own again he'll explore for real while his mother works.

Yesterday she never guessed he stayed so close the whole time, waiting for the afternoon to pass. Today he'll be braver.

They arrive at their destination—not so far, just the island across the way—and he steps out into the water and takes his side of the canoe to help tote it to shore.

He's a real woodsman now. Or a real canoes-man. Whatever it's called.

He's startled, though, when his mother retrieves a furled umbrella from the bottom of the canoe.

"What's that for?" he asks, checking the sky. It's as blue as a robin's egg.

"Just in case," she says with a mysterious smile, and holding the umbrella as if it were a cane, she starts walking.

Ben and Sunshine hurry after.

In case of what? he wonders, and something deep inside him turns over. If his dad said "something special," it would for sure be something he would love. But with his mother . . . well, he hasn't been around her long enough to be certain.

They walk for a while, companionably, no need to talk, until she stops at the edge of a grove of trees. The trees are all the same kind, tall, slender. Long needles gather into tufts along each delicate branch.

"Tamaracks," his mother says. "They're not like most other conifers. The needles turn gold in the autumn and fall off. Then they grow new needles in the spring."

So that's what she brought him to see. Just trees.

His mother hitches herself up onto a large, flat boulder just inside the tamarack grove. "Let's watch for a while," she says. "This is another favorite place."

Ben climbs up, too. *Watch for what?* he wonders. *Favorite for who?* But again he doesn't ask.

Sunshine settles on the ground beneath their feet.

All three of them wait.

After what seems a long time, almost as long as the endless afternoon he spent on the tree-bench yesterday, his mother leans into him, nudging him with her shoulder. "Look!" she whispers.

He looks.

At first he sees nothing. Only trees. The trees she brought him to see. And then . . . something dark. Something very dark. Moving.

More than one something. A second, smaller darkness follows.

And suddenly he knows. His heart begins pounding before his eyes can quite make it out.

Then his eyes know, too.

It's a bear. Two bears! A mama bear with a baby following close behind!

Aren't they the most dangerous? Isn't that what people say? Mama bears with babies?

Ben's body goes taut, a pulled rubber band.

His breath gathers into a knot in the middle of his chest.

The big bear lopes into the thicket, her black fur flowing like water.

Ben squeezes his eyes shut and grips the edge of the boulder. When he opens them again, both bears are still there.

If he stays very still, maybe they will go away.

Then he and his mother will walk to the canoe, paddle to her sturdy cabin, and close the door against mama bears, against baby bears. Against every kind of bear.

At least when he goes home at the end of the week, if he lives to go home, he can tell Russell he saw bears.

Right up close!

And he can tell Russell he wasn't even scared. Not much, anyway.

"Whatever happens," his mother whispers, "don't run."

She has straightened, leaving a gap between them, a gap that feels empty and cold. Ben leans closer, trying to fill it. If she'd just put her arm around him, he wouldn't shrug it off this time. For sure.

But she doesn't. She sits perfectly still, her hands lying loosely in her lap.

The mama bear, the big mama bear, slows to a stop in the middle of the grove. Her baby stops, too. The mama snuffles along the ground for a time, then, just when Ben thinks she's surely ready to move on, she rises to her hind legs, standing just the way a human might stand, and stretches her long body, her long claws, up and up into one of the trees.

She stands that way for a moment as though that's all she means to do, measure her solid bulk against the slender tree. Then to Ben's amazement she begins to climb.

He holds his breath. Where is she going anyway? That skinny tree can't be strong enough to hold her.

The mama bear climbs, and the tree sways.

The mama bear climbs, and her baby stays on the ground.

Up and up and up. Until the tree, overcome

by the weight of the bear, bows almost double and deposits her back onto the ground.

When her baby rushes to greet her, Ben's heart warms at the reunion. This is almost fun. As long as the bears stay far enough away.

A bear capable of climbing that tree could clamber up this boulder in an instant.

Ben's scalp tingles just thinking about it.

This isn't a zoo with bars or fence or glass. This is the real world. These are real bears. And he and his mother are sitting right here without a thing to protect them.

Except his mother's umbrella, whatever that's about.

But the mama bear doesn't like it back on the ground with her baby.

She climbs the tamarack tree again, the same tree that bent under her weight last time. She climbs up and up until, once more, the slender tree bows with her weight and she rides it to the ground.

Then she climbs again.

And again.

It's a game!

Who knew a mama bear could play like that? Who knew the tree would return her to her baby every time?

Ben's body loosens. He looks down to see what Sunshine thinks of bears and their games, but Sunshine isn't thinking. She's moving. Creeping. Her body crouched, her neck stretched long, her tail poked straight out behind, she's inching toward the baby bear on the ground.

"Oh!" Ben gasps. And it's not a whisper. It's a whole loud "OH!"

His mother's hand drops onto his knee.

The baby bear turns at the sound, turns from watching his climbing mother to look in their direction. But he's not looking at them. Ben is sure the baby bear isn't looking at them, sitting high on the boulder. He's looking right at Sunshine!

The baby bear looks and looks, and Sunshine looks, too. But Sunshine doesn't just look. She keeps creeping closer and closer to the baby bear.

"Sunshine!" Ben cries. "DON'T!"

His mother's grip on his knee tightens. "Hush!" she says, fierce but low.

He hushes.

But just then the mama bear drops from the tree again. She chuffs and lumbers over to check on her baby, her head low, swaying. Lumbers over to her baby and to Sunshine, standing so close.

"SUNSHINE!" Ben cries again, ignoring the hand gripping his knee. "SUNSHINE!"

And he leaps off the boulder.

His little dog pays him no mind. Only the mama bear notices. She looks beyond her cub now, even beyond Sunshine, to stare directly at him.

She chuffs again, louder this time, and begins to move. Toward him!

After that, everything happens at once. His mother hops off the boulder and points her umbrella at the approaching bear. She points and pops. The umbrella swooshes open.

And Ben's legs start running.

He can't stop himself. He couldn't stop himself if the whole world had ordered him to stand still. He just races as fast as he can, pushing past tree limbs, stumbling over rocks, charging through brush.

Away from the bears.

Away from Sunshine.

Away from his mother, too.

He runs without once looking back.

When he bursts through the trees to the shore and sees the friendly canoe waiting there, he stops and doubles over, gasping for air, a hand pressed to the stabbing pain in his side.

It takes a long time for his breath to come back, but when it does, he turns to look behind him. Will his mother emerge from those trees? Will Sunshine?

Or will it be the bears?

His body trembling, his breath still coming fast, he shoves the canoe closer to the water. He's ready for escape. At least he didn't get lost in his scramble.

Who knew a popping umbrella could scare a bear? Except he didn't stay around long enough to see if it really did scare her. He just ran.

Exactly what his mother told him not to do.

He ran and left his mother and Sunshine to the bears. Left them to get gobbled up. Not like the brave rescues he performs in his stories.

Ben closes his eyes. If the bear is going to come, even if Sunshine and his mother are going to come, he doesn't want to see.

A rustling in the brush at the edge of the pebble beach.

A voice.

"There you are!"

Ben's eyes pop open. His mother strides toward him, Sunshine following close behind.

"I'm sorry," she says. "That was my fault." But though her words are soft, her eyes are steel sparks and her mouth forms a thin line. "It was entirely my fault," she says again.

She picks up the canoe and carries it into the water without giving him a chance to help.

"That was too much to expect of you," she says. "I've lived among these creatures for so long I forget how fearsome they seem."

Sunshine is saying she's sorry, too, bumping her cool nose against his leg. My *fault*, the bump says. My *fault. I shouldn't have gone to check the baby bear.*

His mother settles the canoe on the water and tosses his life jacket to him. She drops the furled umbrella into the bottom of the canoe. "The umbrella did its work," she says. "Most folks use bear spray, but spray stings their eyes. A popping umbrella startles them, and they go away. Nobody hurt."

She's right. Of course. Nobody was hurt. Not the bears. Not them. Not even Sunshine, who was in the most danger of all. But that doesn't mean everything is all right.

Something very big is wrong.

Him.

He shouted at Sunshine when his mother told him to be quiet. He ran when she told him not to run.

What more could he do to spoil his plan?

CHAPTER 9
Doing Okay

Ben's mother sets the sandwich in front of him. Ham and cheese again. Crisp and melty again, too.

"Thank you," he says.

She nods, then sits across from him, folding her hands on the table. She hasn't even brought a rolled-up tube of ham and cheese for her own lunch. Clearly she has something on her mind other than eating.

Talking, no doubt.

Ben is pretty sure he doesn't want to hear whatever she's planning to say. Just because she pretended everything was her fault doesn't mean she's not unhappy with him.

And what can he say? *I never told my legs to run? Just like I didn't tell my shoulder to shrug you away?*

"Ben," his mother says, "I think we need to talk about Sunshine."

His head pops up, and he finds himself looking into the flecks of gold in her eyes. And into the seriousness in those eyes.

This isn't what he expected.

"She's my spirit animal," he says. "That's all. There's nothing wrong with having a spirit animal. You said."

"There's nothing wrong," she agrees. "But maybe it's time—"

"NO!"

She studies him for a long moment, her head tipped to one side. "No what?" she asks.

"I'm not too old. Not too old to have an imagin—" He starts again. "I'm not too old to have a *daemon*." He leans hard on the word.

"I see," she says, though he has no idea what that means. Then she adds, "I agree. You aren't too old."

Ben's shoulders have risen until they practically cover his ears, and now they fall again. Still, whatever she has to say about Sunshine, he's sure he's not going to like it.

When she doesn't say anything more, he takes a big bite out of his sandwich. He bites, chews, swallows. Once he finishes eating, he can get away from those watching eyes. Get away from talking about Sunshine, too.

But then she starts up again. "Maybe it's time to look at what your *daemon*"—she leans hard on the word, too—"is about. Where she comes from. Time to look at things straight on."

Ben has no idea what she's talking about except that it sounds like another way of telling him he's too old for an imaginary dog. And it doesn't matter who says it or how they dress it up, he's not giving up Sunshine. She makes him feel . . . What is it that she makes him feel?

Safe.

He stands. "Sunshine isn't *about* anything," he says. "She just *is*." Then, before his mother can say more, he adds, "We're going outside now. To explore. So you can work on your novel."

But she holds a hand out, palm down. *Sit*, the hand says. And he sits.

His mother takes a breath. Almost as though she's getting ready to plunge into deep water. "Do you remember Mrs. Schwartz?" she asks. "Our next-door neighbor?"

Ben remembers. Sort of. Mrs. Schwartz was an old lady. A nice old lady. She moved away a long time ago. Not as long ago as his mother, though.

Nobody has been gone as long as his mother.

He nods, but even as he does, he wonders. What does Mrs. Schwartz have to do with anything? He thought they were going to talk about Sunshine.

"And do you remember Shadow? Mrs. Schwartz's Cavalier King Charles spaniel?"

"Her cav . . . what?"

"Her Cavalier King Charles spaniel," she says again. She says it patiently, as though she's talking to someone very young. Or a little bit stupid. "That's the kind of dog Mrs. Schwartz had. A Cavalier is a small spaniel with a long tail and a short nose. They've been bred for centuries as companion dogs."

He shakes his head. She keeps going.

"How you loved Shadow! I've never seen a little boy love a dog more. He was black and tan."

Ben tries to remember a black-and-tan dog. He can't.

"What color is Sunshine?" his mother asks.

Back when his dad used to be willing to talk about Sunshine, there was always a certain tone in his voice. A tone that implied, "Isn't it fun to pretend?" His mother's question comes washed clean of any tone. They might be talking about the table in front of them.

"Red," he answers. "Kind of a coppery red." He glances at his mother's hair as he says it. He can't help it. But he looks away again just as fast.

She nods. "Then Sunshine is a ruby. That's what they call red Cavaliers. And if I'm not mistaken, that's what she is. A Cavalier."

Ben has never thought about his dog's being anything . . . except just Sunshine. And if there was once a real dog that was the model for Sunshine, he's forgotten it entirely.

He presses a fingertip to his plate, gathering the last crisp crumbs left from his sandwich, then touches the finger to his tongue. He looks at his mother straight on.

"Don't worry," he says. "I know I made her up. Like I told you, she's just a story."

"Just a story," his mother repeats in a musing way. "I can't think of much that's more important than the stories we tell ourselves."

But Ben has had enough. He doesn't want to hear his mother talk about Sunshine. Or about stories, either. He stands again. "Sunshine's mine," he says. "All mine. She's got nothing to do with you! I don't know why you keep on about her."

His mother holds his gaze for a long moment. Then she nods. That quick little nod of hers that says something is finished. At least for now.

He heads outside. Just the way he said he would. To give his mother the afternoon with her own silly story.

———◎———

Ben sits at the edge of the lake just beyond the cabin and the outhouse for a long time, listening to the steady lapping of the waves against the shore.

What was his mother talking about in there anyway? So what if their neighbor had a . . . what was it called? A cavalier, a king . . . something. Who cares? Sunshine is his. And nobody in the whole world can take her away. Not by telling him he's too old. Not by telling him there was another dog like her, either.

Sunshine has followed him out and sits next to the overturned canoe again, gazing across the lake. That's all she seems to think about these days, going out in the canoe.

Or sniffing baby bears.

Ben looks out across the water, too. It does look nice out there. Almost nice enough to want to be paddling again.

He holds that idea close for a moment. There are, after all, lots of ways to explore.

He walks slowly to the canoe, squats and peers underneath. Is it possible? Yes. The paddles are there. The life jackets, too.

He straightens, the idea rising within him like the morning sun. He knows how to paddle a canoe, doesn't he? And if he explores by canoe, he won't risk getting lost in a maze of trees. The whole time he's out there, he'll be able to look back to see where he came from, look ahead to see where he's going.

And wouldn't a little outing in the canoe be better than sitting here for the whole long afternoon the way he did yesterday?

Besides, his mother would be pleased to know he's brave enough to paddle a canoe all by himself. Maybe she'd even forget about his running away from the bears. Maybe she'd forget about the way he cried "wolf" about the loons, too.

Ben flips the canoe over, then stands back to study it. Narrow and long. Real long. Can he steer it the way his mother did? Without any help?

He doesn't have to call Sunshine to join him. The minute he turned the canoe upright, she installed herself in the bow. "You're right," he says, nodding to her. "Let's go."

He puts on his life jacket, noticing as he zips it

up how well it fits. His mother must have bought a life jacket just for him. He hadn't thought about that before, that she wouldn't need a child-sized life jacket except for him.

He picks up a paddle and drops it into the bottom. He considers taking the second one, too. Just in case Sunshine wants to help. He smiles at the thought, but he leaves the second paddle on the ground.

It will mark the exact spot where he will return the canoe.

He tries lifting the canoe to carry it the way his mother would, but without her on the other side he can't get it even an inch off the ground. So he shoves instead.

When he gets to the water, he wades in, pushing the canoe before him. His feet go instantly numb in the icy water, and his breath catches high in his chest. He climbs in, setting the canoe rocking wildly so that he has to grab on to the sides and wait to see if they are going to capsize.

When all goes still again, he picks up the

paddle. One hand at the top, the other below. His hands remember the position easily now. The sore place at the base of his thumb remembers, too.

A long, flat bird floating on the water studies him with a startlingly red eye. Black-and-white checks. Black head. Long, pointed beak. It must be a loon. He's seen pictures.

But pictures don't make that crazy sound.

He's grateful for the loon's silence now. Even knowing it's not a wolf, he doesn't want to hear that eerie cry. He's glad to know he's not the only one that sound ever scared, but still . . .

He glances back over his shoulder. Not a trace of movement from the cabin.

He dips the paddle and the canoe slides forward. He does it again.

The canoe cuts through the water, silent and smooth. He likes the silent movement. Likes it especially now that he's the one making it happen. Just him. Alone.

Well, him and Sunshine together.

"We're off!" he announces to his ship's figure-head.

And they are.

With each thrust of the paddle, though, the canoe zigzags wildly. How does his mother keep this thing going straight? If he didn't switch sides with every stroke, he would be going in circles.

There must be something about steering a canoe that she hasn't taught him.

His hands shake, his brain buzzes, but he keeps at it.

When he's out a short distance, he looks back, half expecting to see his mother standing on the shore, calling him to return. Half wanting to see her standing there.

No one. Which proves she doesn't care that he's taking her canoe. She's too busy thinking about her novel to care.

That's her island he's looking at, though. Right behind him. The rocky shore, the towering trees, the green, the green, the green. But it looks exactly like every other shore he can see from here, every shore they passed along the way. He'll have to be careful to keep it behind him so he has only to turn around to get back.

When his arms get tired, he lifts the paddle out of the water and holds it across his lap. The breeze pushes against his back, keeping the canoe moving. If he wanted to, he could just sit here perfectly still and be blown to the island across the way. The one where they saw the bears.

The one where Sunshine wants to go.

He's not dumb enough to do that, though. He doesn't even have an umbrella! He smiles at the thought.

Just wait until he tells Russell about the way his mother popped an umbrella in the face of a charging bear!

When the opposite shore gets closer, he consults Sunshine. "Time to go back?" he says. "Don't you think?"

To his astonishment, she answers. "Let's keep going!" she says. And she tips her head to indicate the island they are approaching.

Ben almost drops the paddle.

"You can't talk!" he cries. "You've never, ever talked!"

"Okay," she replies, agreeably, and she goes

back to staring off in the direction she just told him to take.

Ben's heart pounds. Sunshine spoke to him! His dog spoke to him! She's never done that before. Not once. Talking isn't in the rules for being a dog. Hearing words come out of her mouth makes him feel . . . well, strange.

His mother said Sunshine is his story. What do they call people when their stories get so real they start talking back? Crazy?

"Don't do that again," he tells her. And he half expects her to say okay once more, but she doesn't. She doesn't even look at him. But the way she keeps her focus on the shore across the way still says it as clearly as any words.

Let's keep going.

Ben dips the paddle. He can go just a bit closer before he turns around. Close enough to make Sunshine happy.

A bald eagle wheels against the sky. White head, white under its tail. His mother taught him how to identify a bald eagle on their way here. The big bird holds so still, the stretched wings never flapping, that it seems unreal, like something painted against the blue of the sky.

Almost as unreal as a talking dog.

Ben's heart has settled back into its usual gentle rhythm, so quiet as not to be noticed. Quiet the way the paddle is quiet, the small swish it makes each time he dips into the water, each time it pulls them forward.

The canoe still goes off at an angle with each stroke, but when he changes sides, he can make it angle back again, so they're going pretty straight. With the wind's help.

"We're doing okay, you and me. Don't you think?" he says to his daemon.

To his relief, she doesn't bother to reply.

He dips the paddle again, draws the canoe to the paddle. He dips and dips.

CHAPTER 10
All by Himself

As the canoe approaches the opposite shore, Sun-shine leans forward over the bow.

"No you don't," Ben tells her, stopping pad-dling. "No more bear hunts."

But the wind that's been such a friendly help on the way over here is no help at all now. He bends over, paddling backward fiercely all on the same side, but the canoe turns away from the bears' island with excruciating slowness. He stops to rest his arms just for an instant, and the wind pivots the canoe back again.

He paddles harder, turning away again.

When he straightens from his exertions, he no longer has a ship's figurehead in the bow. Sunshine has disappeared completely.

"Sunshine!" he calls, whipping around to check the shore where he had come with no intention of landing.

And there she is, trotting along the beach, heading straight for the woods. How did she get there?

"Sunshine!" he calls.

His voice fills the arching sky, but Sunshine doesn't seem to hear. Or if she does, she's ignoring him. She disappears into the undergrowth.

Ben goes limp, staring at the spot where he saw the last flash of reddish-gold tail.

As he sits, no longer paddling, the wind doesn't just take hold and turn the canoe, neatly and efficiently, back toward the bears' island again. It bumps him into the shore. He climbs out, dragging the canoe behind him, pulling it just far enough out of the water to keep it from floating away.

Then he stands on the shore and calls again. "Sunshine!"

The rocky shore, the wall of trees, the clouds sailing overhead . . . everything swallows his voice.

He kicks a rock that's lying there, just waiting to be kicked. The rock barely moves, but his toe throbs.

And that's when he sees it. Right there. In the dried mud. A single footprint.

It looks like a print a human might leave behind. A very large human with bare feet. Except for the deep indentation at the end of each toe. Indentations that could have been made only by claws.

Ben doesn't know a thing about animal tracks. But having seen the bears this morning, he knows. This was made by a bear. A large one.

He didn't need a reminder of what's on this island, but now that he has one, he turns back, pushes the canoe into the water, climbs in, and begins paddling again. Away.

So Sunshine has decided to leave him. Why

should he care? Let her do what she wants.

It's what she's good at lately.

His mother's island is right over there. Not as close as he'd like it to be, but he certainly doesn't need help from an imaginary dog to find it.

He applies the paddle to the water just the way his mother taught him, drawing the canoe to the paddle. Then he does it again. And again.

At first he likes the feel of facing into the wind. The air riffles through his hair as though he's coasting down a hill on his bike. It doesn't take long, though, for him to realize that the brisk breeze that helped bring him here now holds him back. He can move forward if he paddles steadily, but his progress is excruciatingly slow.

He digs deeper, pushes harder. The sore spots at the base of his thumbs had been hard and red when he started out. Now they erupt into blisters. First closed blisters and then open ones. Open and stinging.

And with the wind against him, it's even more difficult this time to keep going straight.

He stops paddling for a moment to shade his

eyes with a hand. He can't see his mother's cabin from here. He can't even see her outhouse. But then the trees are so heavy, it's difficult to make out either building even when he's right on the shore. It never occurred to him when he paddled away that it might be as hard to figure out where to land as it would have been to make his way back through the tangle of trees.

He starts paddling again before the wind can blow him back to the bears.

He can't even guess what time it is. One instant the sun was shining, and in the next a heavy blanket of clouds moved in, hiding the sun completely.

Has he been gone long enough for his mother to begin to worry?

Maybe a little worry won't hurt her. His dad worries about him all the time. Is he dressed warmly enough? Is he keeping up with math? If he eats another piece of pie, will he get a tummy ache?

It's only fair for his mother to take her turn.

A sudden gust, stronger than the steady wind he has been plowing into, lifts the bow right out of the water and rocks the canoe wildly. Ben digs harder with the paddle, trying to stay steady, trying to keep pointing the right way.

Which would be worse? To be eaten by bears or to capsize and drown? He's wearing his life jacket, but a person can die of hypo . . . something. It's when you die of cold. Everybody in Minnesota has heard of hypo . . . whatever it is.

What will his mother say to his father if he doesn't come back? Will she have to admit she lied when she promised no emergencies?

And Sunshine. What will happen to Sunshine? Without him to live inside, she'll be gone, too.

Despite his dark thoughts, despite the cold water that sloshes into the canoe with the heavier gusts, Ben's paddling makes progress. Slow, but progress. He's nearly halfway there. A great shiver passes through him from the chill of the wetting that comes with that sloshing water. From fear, too. From terror, really. Gradually, gradually, though, his mother's island does move closer.

Or rather he moves closer to the island. Her island does nothing to help.

Another gust, harder than any of the rest, sets

the canoe rocking so wildly that Ben grabs for the sides, dropping the paddle. He lunges and grabs it back from the water almost before he realizes he's dropped it.

For a few seconds, he sits utterly still, pressing the dripping thing against his chest. What would happen to him if he lost the paddle? His mother doesn't even have another canoe to come looking for him.

And while he's cradling the paddle, the wind takes hold, spinning the canoe. He goes around once. Twice. Three times?

"Sunshine!" he cries, as though she were here, as though she could help if she were.

He begins paddling again, but then he stops. He gazes at the rocky green shore ahead, turns back to study the rocky green shore behind. How many times did the wind turn him? Which island is he facing now?

He can't tell one shore from the other!

Even as he sits staring, trying to decide which direction to go, the wind turns the canoe again.

Nothing to do but make a choice and paddle.

So he decides. That one! And he starts in again.

It seems to be getting easier, this paddling business. Maybe he's getting better.

But when he nudges the canoe once more into the shore and climbs out, tugging the clumsy thing after him, he stops cold.

There it is again. The footprint. With the deep imprint of a claw at the end of each toe. The footprint of the bear! Amazing that he returned, not just to the same island but to the exact same place.

He should have noticed that he was paddling with the wind instead of against it, but he was so scared he wasn't noticing anything.

"Sunshine!" he calls, one last time. But she doesn't come.

Without wasting another minute, he pushes the canoe into the water and sets out again. His arms have gone curiously weak, but at least he knows which way to go now. This time he's not going to stop paddling until he's safe.

He still can't tell whether he's heading for the right place on his mother's island, but at least he's certain he's headed for the right island. Getting to any part of it will be better than being here with the bears.

With the bears and with Sunshine, who loves bears more than she loves him.

He paddles and paddles. If he's drawing closer, he can hardly tell.

He would take his arms off and lay them down in the bottom of the canoe if he could. He would throw his stinging hands away if that were possible, too. But since he can't do either and since no one is here to help—not even his daemon—he rides the swells of the slapping waves, pushing again and again with the hateful paddle.

He's a paddling machine. No thoughts. No hopes, even. Just hands and arms, shoulders and back. And the paddle. Again and again and again, the paddle.

The wind seems to be rising, and about every third wave rushing toward him now has a frothy white cap. Sometimes the froth tumbles into the canoe and dances at his feet.

His feet were soaked anyway, but now his legs are wet, too, and even his body. The wind, without any sun to warm it, chills him through and through.

When at last the canoe bumps into the shore, Ben can't stop paddling. He keeps right on, pushing, pushing, not caring what is scratched, just wanting dry land beneath him. Just wanting to be home.

Well, not home.

Just wanting to be back at his mother's cabin. Back where an adult is in charge.

When the canoe is as far onto the shore as he can force it by paddling, he climbs out and drags the thing from the water.

Then he collapses onto the pebbly beach.

He made it! He got back to his mother's island. It's the bravest thing he's ever done, and he did it all by himself, too.

Sunshine didn't help even a little bit.

Chapter 11
Did You Have Fun?

The beach is dry, but the rocks are hard, and one, sharper and bigger than the rest, presses into Ben's side. He sits up and looks around.

Sunshine is beside him, gazing at him. He looks away from those love-you-forever eyes. Why does she show up now? When he doesn't need her. Doesn't need her at all.

He studies his surroundings. He can't see a single sign of his mother's cabin from here . . . wherever *here* is.

How big is this island anyway? He never asked,

and since he didn't explore yesterday, he has no idea. But it feels enormous.

Dumb. Really, truly dumb. If his father were here, he would turn into his teacher self and point out all the bad choices Ben made. He would talk and talk about it until Ben's brain wanted to explode.

Will his mother do the same?

She'll be worried, that's for sure. And if she's worried, she's going to be angry. That's when his dad really gets mad, when Ben has worried him. Once Ben and Russell went off on their bikes and got so lost that they didn't get back until after dark. When they finally showed up, Dad hugged them both so hard they could barely breathe. Then he nearly took their heads off.

Anyway, even if his mother is mad, he has to get back to her, and he has to do it now.

He stands and looks around. He can see rocks and trees, bushes and water, the same rocks and trees and bushes and water that exist everywhere in this wilderness. If only he could tell which direction to go to reach the cabin. *That way!* he thinks, looking off to his right. But when he turns around, he's no longer sure. It might be the other way.

Great. He has two directions to choose from, and one looks no more likely than the other.

He sits down again and stares at Sunshine. She offers nothing, just a soulful look and a slow wag of her tail.

If she were one of those dogs they write about in stories, she never would have gone off looking for baby bears. She would have stayed by his side every minute. And if she were one of those story dogs, when the wind got too strong for him to steer properly, she would have jumped out, taken the mooring rope between her teeth, and pulled him, canoe and all, to the place on the shore closest to his mother's cabin.

At the very least, she should be barking now, barking and showing him the way. Not just sitting there waiting for him to figure everything out by himself.

His father is right. He's too old for this "imaginary friend" nonsense.

"Get!" he says to the little dog. "Go away!" he says to her sappy, adoring gaze. And he picks up a handful of pebbles and tosses them at her.

Sunshine's surprise melts instantly into hurt. Her ears go flat and her head droops. Then she stands, shakes off the insult of the pebbles, and slinks away, her tail tucked between her legs. When she's out of reach even of tossed pebbles, she turns back to give him a long, studying look. *You don't really mean it, do you?* the look says.

Whatever she gathers from his face, she keeps going.

Ben doesn't care. If she can't stick around when he really needs her, what's the point of having a daemon anyway?

He's empty. Not just hungry empty, though he's hungry, too. Alone-in-the-world, never-going-to-be-filled empty.

Still, sitting here isn't doing him any good. He lunges to his feet, chooses a direction, and heads out.

Maybe he'll even find Sunshine again along the way.

Not that he cares.

Ben stays close to the lake as he walks to keep from getting turned around. Or lost among the trees. Surely he'll be able to see the cabin from the shore. Or if not the cabin, at least the outhouse.

Walking isn't much easier than paddling against the wind. There is no path and the way is uneven. Boulders spring up in front of him. Trees grow right down to the water, their gnarly roots humping into the air, daring him to pass.

Still he persists, tromping what seems a great distance without once seeing any sign of the cabin. When he's pretty certain he's walked farther than he could have been blown away from his starting point, he returns to base camp—the canoe—and starts out again in the other direction. He's beginning to stumble over pebbles.

The second time he returns to the canoe, he's so relieved to see something familiar, something that isn't just more wilderness, that he collapses onto the ground next to it. If the darn thing weren't so big and clunky, he'd hug it.

Sunshine is still nowhere to be seen.

This time her absence leaves a hole the size of the Grand Canyon. Ben and his dad drove all the way to see the Grand Canyon last summer, so he knows what a big hole that is. And that's how big it feels, having her gone.

He closes his eyes, squeezes them shut, and thinks, *Sunshine!* He thinks it hard, hard, but when his eyes come open again . . . nothing.

Okay. If that's the way she's going to be.

But he can't help himself. He keeps looking for her anyway. Keeps looking, but not seeing.

He can't sit here waiting for a pretend dog to save him, though. He has to figure out what to do on his own.

Surely it's past suppertime. His stomach certainly thinks so. The sun has dropped almost to the treetops. His mother will have quit working on her novel by now and come out to look for him. She'll see that he is gone. Her canoe, too.

She'll know that all kinds of bad things could happen to a boy out on this enormous gray lake by himself. And she can't even come looking for him, because he took her canoe. She has no way even to paddle into town to call his dad.

She'll be worried. That's for sure. And really, really mad!

The waves tumble into the shore with a resounding *slap-bang*.

Now that Ben has quit walking, can't possibly walk any farther, he's beginning to shiver, great rolling bursts that set his teeth clacking.

Why did he think exploring in the canoe was a good idea anyway? Because he couldn't get lost? It's almost enough to make him laugh. Almost.

Another shiver hits him so hard that he can practically feel his bones knock together.

He reaches into the canoe and feels around on the bottom. Maybe there is something that will help in there—a blanket, a hoodie, a jacket. Not that he expects to find anything. If there had been anything useful in the canoe, he would have spotted it long ago. And it would be soaking wet, too.

Just like him.

Last he feels the underside of the bench, and his hand comes across something hard. A box? A metal box!

He dislodges it, turns it over, pries the latch open.

First-aid supplies. Band-Aids, disinfectant, aspirin, safety pins, tweezers. An ACE bandage. Bug spray. Nothing that will help. He doesn't even need the bug spray. The wind is blowing hard enough that the insects can't fly.

Maybe he could use the disinfectant and Band-Aids for his blistered hands. But what he needs most is something to keep him warm . . . and something to eat. There's nothing for either in here. You'd think his mother would at least have included something to eat in her emergency box.

He dumps the contents of the box into the bottom of the canoe, and a small metal cylinder tumbles out. Opened, it reveals matches.

At least he can start a fire to get warm.

Just holding the matches in his hand gives him the energy to stand, even to wander around a bit gathering twigs, brush, a pile of dead pine needles. There are dead pine needles everywhere. His mother said last night that it's been an unusually dry spring. Not as much snowmelt as usual and not as much rain. So a fire shouldn't be hard to get going.

A strike pad at the bottom of the tiny canister gives him something to scratch a match against, and by the third match, the fire takes hold. The small, shining flame climbs the twigs he has propped against one another to give the fire air. He learned that from Russell's dad. He taught them how to make a campfire in Russell's backyard so they can roast hot dogs and marshmallows.

In seconds, the flame drops to the needles at the base of the twigs and begins to burn cheerfully.

Ben goes to look for larger wood, something that can give out more heat. Maybe once the fire gets going, he can figure out a way to send smoke signals. His woodswoman mother is probably one of the few people left in the world who can read smoke signals. If only he knew how to say "Come get me!" in puffs of smoke.

But by the time he gets back with an armload

of dead wood, the flame has burned itself out. He drops the wood and hunkers down in front of the charred twigs, cupping his hands around them and blowing gently.

A spark springs to life. Just one small spark.

Another puff sets the needles at the base of the twigs glowing. He adds more dry pine needles, more twigs, slowly, slowly. When they catch, he props some of the dead wood over the burning twigs.

The flame sputters, fades, then gathers again. But it isn't putting out much heat.

He sits back on his heels.

This is too hard. Even if he can get the fire going, staying here isn't the answer.

If he doesn't find his mother's cabin, he'll be spending the night in the forest. With no cover and this little campfire his only protection against the cold.

Thunder rumbles in the distance.

If it rains, he won't even have the fire!

Then there are those bears on the island just across the way. The bears he's already seen. What if they decide to swim over here? Or maybe there are more bears on this island!

His mother said there are wolves up here, too. Real wolves. Not just the loons that sound like wolves.

By the time he remembers there are still moose in northern Minnesota, too—like the one his mother saw—and that they have a reputation for being pretty cranky, he is on his feet. It doesn't matter how tired he is. He's got to keep looking for the cabin.

It can't be far away. But which way? Why couldn't he find it before?

Maybe he wasn't looking hard enough. Whichever way he walked, he kept thinking it must be the other way, so maybe he wasn't really looking.

He stands still, the wind riffling through his hair.

And then he knows. The wind isn't just blowing straight, from this island to the bear island across the way. It's blowing between the islands at an angle, coming a bit more from *that* way. He faces into it. It would have blown him in the opposite direction.

If he walks against the wind that was pushing him, he'll be going toward the cabin.

See! He doesn't need Sunshine. He can figure things out on his own!

He starts walking again, but he doesn't get very far before he stops and looks back. At the canoe. What will his mother say if he comes back without her canoe? He looks at the fire, too. It's beginning to take hold. He shouldn't leave the fire burning.

He has nothing to carry water in to put out the fire, but he goes back, scatters the burning sticks, and kicks dirt over everything. A thick blanket of dirt. He stomps on it, too.

He kicks and stomps until he can no longer see even a trace of smoke.

Then he goes to the canoe, puts on his life vest, pushes the canoe into the water, and climbs in. He'll go back the way he left, in the canoe. Then his mother will be proud of him for sure.

She told to him to explore, didn't she? And that's what he did. She didn't say he was supposed to stay on the island, though now that he thinks about it, that's probably what she meant.

Paddling hard, Ben stays close to the shore. As he paddles, he can't stop himself from sneaking peeks at the bow, expecting Sunshine to show up. She doesn't.

He doesn't care, though. What does he need with an imaginary dog? He's finding his own way.

When he catches a glimpse of a shingled roof through the trees, his heart soars. The outhouse! He never thought he would be so glad to see the outhouse. He doesn't know why he didn't see it earlier, but there it is.

He's done it! He's back!

Ben bumps the canoe into the shore and climbs out. He slows himself down enough to stow the first-aid kit, then pulls the canoe well up onto the shore and flips it over the way his mother would.

Exhausted as he is, he begins to run.

He's back! He's back! His mother is going to be angry, but that's all right. That's what parents do when you worry them too badly. First, they're relieved, and then, almost on top of it, they're really, really mad.

All he has to do is get through the mad and then everything will be fine.

Ben slams through the door, panting. He stops in the middle of the floor.

His mother is at the table, right where he left her when he went off after lunch. In fact, the lunch dishes—the breakfast ones, too—are still there, just pushed to one side. And she is just sitting, her head lowered over one of those notebooks of hers, a lit lantern beside her.

She looks up, pen in hand.

"Well, hello," she says, giving him a slightly fuzzy smile, as though she's been pulled back from some other world and isn't quite at home in this one yet. "Did you have fun exploring?"

Ben stares. Not only was she not worried. Not only is she not angry. His mother—his very own mother—didn't even notice how long he'd been gone.

He slams down onto the bench across from her

at the table, his own anger, the anger she accused him of earlier, burning in his veins.

"Yeah," he says, his words heavy with sarcasm. "I had great fun."

She looks at him. Looks right at him. But she doesn't get it. Not at all.

"I'll bet you're hungry," she says, and she rises from the table. "I got a lot of work done this afternoon, but I made some soup, too."

He says nothing. What is there to say?

Chapter 12
To Keep You Safe

Ben peers into the bowl that has appeared in front of him on the table. His heart is still hammering, but he pretends calm. The contents of the bowl, whatever they are, look brown and ugly. It looks like . . .

He doesn't want to think about what it looks like.

"Lentil soup," his mother says.

In response to his inquiring glance, she explains. "Lentils are the queen of beans. They're tiny and filled with protein."

Ugh! Beans! He doesn't like beans any more than he likes pickles.

His stomach rumbles, though, and his hand reaches for the spoon. The spoon hovers over the brown mess without actually dipping into it.

How could she not have noticed he wasn't here? June days are long in Minnesota. Really long. And the high windows in the cabin have grown nearly dark. Which means it's closer to bedtime than suppertime.

If he hadn't come back at all, would she have noticed then?

He stirs the brown sludge of beans.

So much could have happened.

If he hadn't recovered the paddle when he dropped it, he could have been blown to the other end of this enormous lake. Maybe never found. Or if he'd tipped the canoe, he could have died of hypo . . . whatever.

Even after he got back to his mother's island, he might never have found his way to the cabin. He could still be out there wandering. Or trying to use his dinky campfire to keep warm through the night, to keep wild animals away.

And here she sat the whole time, working on

her silly novel. Not even thinking about him. Not even caring!

"Did you get a lot of writing done?" he asks, his words marching out, stiff as soldiers.

She smiles as though it's a real question, one he wants an answer to. "Not a lot of actual writing," she says. "But I worked through a stuck place, and I'm moving again. So it was good. The time you gave me was well spent."

She tips her head to one side, and for an instant he catches a glimpse of a little girl peering out of her eyes. A happy little girl.

"What about you?" she asks. "What kind of exploring did you do?"

He shrugs. "Not much," he says. Then he adds, "I got lost."

The happy little girl vanishes.

"The wind blew the canoe so hard I couldn't get back to where I started. I didn't think I was ever going to find your cabin again." He says all this in a calm, flat voice. Facts. Just the facts.

"Wait!" Her mouth has dropped open. "You

mean you actually took my canoe out? By yourself? I didn't give you permission to do that!"

"You told me to explore." It's an accusation. Her fault. All that happened this afternoon was her fault.

"Yes . . . I did . . . But, Ben! Surely you knew I didn't mean—"

She stops, shakes her head, starts again. "When I think what could have happened!"

She's gripping the edge of the table, her knuckles shining like pearls. That whitened grip almost makes him feel better. Almost.

"You could have capsized!" she says. Her voice comes out tight, high. "Do you know what could have happened if you'd capsized? You've heard of hypothermia, haven't you?"

So that's what it's called. Hypothermia.

She shakes her head, says it again. "Ben! If you'd fallen into the lake, even with your life jacket on, you could have died of hypothermia!"

The spoon slips out of his hand into the soup. He pays no attention to the spoon, just keeps looking at her. "Would you have noticed if I did?" he asks.

His mother jerks upright as though she's been slapped, but she doesn't answer.

He doesn't like looking at that slapped face, so he concentrates on fishing his dropped spoon out of his brown soup.

When she finally speaks, her voice is so soft he has to replay it inside his head to know what he's heard. "I would have done more than notice, Ben," she says. "I would have broken in two."

The thought fills him with bitter satisfaction. He likes the idea of his mother caring so much that she could break. He likes it very much.

Still . . . it's too late for stuff like that. She can't make him be sorry. She's the one who ought to be sorry.

He leans over his bowl, takes a tentative taste of the soup. Just so he doesn't have to say anything.

The stuff isn't as bad as it looks.

His mother's hands still grip the edge of the table. Like her hands are waiting, too.

The hands release. Fold. Unfold. One finger picks at an invisible speck on the table. Funny that she cares about the speck when the whole thing is littered with books, with notebooks and pens, with dishes from past meals.

Dad would never serve a meal on such a messy table.

Ben sneaks a glance. Except for her freckles and two bright patches of color mottling her cheeks, his mother's face has gone white.

But he's doesn't care about her white face, either. This woman went off and left him. Left and never came back. Not even for his birthday or Christmas. Not even for a good-night hug.

He used to ask Dad about her. *Why?* he asked again and again. *Why did she go?*

And his father, who always answers questions, any question, anytime; his father who explained things to him like how babies are made when other kids were still trying to figure out Santa Claus, that same father said only, "She needed to find something, Ben. Herself, I think."

But that makes no sense. Why run off to an island searching for something she could have found by looking in a mirror?

"She loves you." Dad always said that, too. "You've got to know that she loves you."

And that doesn't make sense, either. How can somebody love you and still go away? And stay! Forever!

"Ben," his mother says. His name comes out like a sigh. "What if I'd had to call your father to tell him—"

Her voice breaks.

So that's what she's so upset about. Not about losing him. She's thinking about the call she would have had to make. How embarrassing it would be to admit that her promise of "no emergencies" was a lie.

"You couldn't have called him anyway," he says. "I had your canoe."

She laughs, but her laugh hasn't even a touch of humor. "You're right about that," she says. "I would have been up the proverbial creek without a paddle."

He's not sure what she means by that, so he

says, "You had a paddle. I left you the other one."

She laughs again. Lighter this time, but still tinged with sadness. "Without a canoe, then."

After that she sits there, silent. She's watching him, though. He can tell she's watching him. He can feel her gaze pressing into his scalp.

He goes back to eating the soup-sludge. He can't help himself. He's starving.

He's almost scraped the bowl clean before she speaks again. "What do you want from me, Ben?" she asks.

The question surprises him into looking at her, really looking at her.

She looks crumpled . . . and not the least bit pretty. Why did he think her hair was red-gold? In the light from the gas lamp on the table, it is brown. Just plain brown. Her eyes looking back at him are plain brown, too. He must have imagined the gold flecks.

She's really asking what he wants?

He wants what he's always wanted. For her to come home so he can have a mother. What else is there to want?

When the words emerge, he bites them off, clean and sharp, but they aren't what he thought he was going to say. What comes out is "Why?"

"Why what?"

"I want to know why you went away."

"Oh," she says, and the "oh" is faint. He might have thrown water on the Wicked Witch of the West. She seems to be melting before his eyes. He isn't sure whether to be relieved or sad at the melting.

She says nothing more. Just that very small "oh."

He waits, holding her with his gaze. He's been waiting for the answer to that question since he was three years old. He can wait a few more minutes. An hour. As long as it takes.

At last she clears her throat. "I left . . ." She licks her lips. "I had to leave . . ."

Her voice trails off and doesn't start up again. As though "I had to leave" explains anything.

Ben begins to count the freckles scattered like stars across his mother's forehead.

She lifts her chin. "I had to leave," she repeats, more forcefully, "to keep you safe."

"To keep me safe?" he asks. Demands, really. "Safe from what?"

And when she presses her lips together and doesn't reply, he realizes he knows the answer already.

Still, he asks again.

"Safe from who?" he says this time.

His mother takes a deep breath before she answers. Then she says it. Says the thing he's known all along.

"Safe from me."

Ben stands, pushes the wooden bench away so that it grates across the floor, walks to the loft ladder. He's a robot moving by some distant command. He doesn't even look at her, just climbs without looking down, without noticing that he is climbing. He crawls onto the platform floor and drops on top of the sleeping bag.

Only the earth-and-pine scent of the sleeping bag reminds him that he is not a robot. He is flesh and blood. A living creature in a world of living creatures.

He lies perfectly still for a long time, listening

for what his mother is going to do. Will she follow him up here? Will she try to explain?

But she doesn't. She doesn't do a thing. At least nothing he can hear. The room below, the tiny cabin, and the wilderness that surrounds the cabin remain silent.

And then, though he hasn't called her, hasn't thought about her even once since he got back, Sunshine is there. Sniffing his face. Licking his cheek. Licking and licking.

That's the only reason his cheek is wet. All that licking.

He sure as heck isn't crying.

But when he feels around with his hand, he can't locate her. No fur. No damp nose. Not even a single long, warm, fluffy ear.

Because he sent her away. Sunshine is gone. Just like his mother has been gone for most of his life.

His mother, who left to keep him safe.

From her.

CHAPTER 13
His Fault

"Ben! Wake up!"

Ben gasps, struggles to sit up, falls back again, too confined by the sleeping bag twisted around him to get himself upright.

"Ben!" A figure leaning over him in the dark, hands on his shoulders. His mother, leaning. Is she going to hurt him? Now?

"Don't!" he cries. "Please!"

Her grip on his shoulders tightens. She gives him a shake.

"Wake up!" she says again. Her words, sharp

and hard. Like blows. "Get your clothes on. Come downstairs. Quick! Quick!"

And she's gone. A light from below throws her shadow across the loft, enormous and dark, as she disappears over the edge.

What is it? What's wrong? Ben's gaze roams the loft, but he can make out nothing but shadows.

He can smell something, though. Smoke! Is that smoke?

He scrambles out of the sleeping bag, pats the floor to find his jeans, his shirt, his wet sneakers.

He has his clothes on now, and his foot seeks out the top rung of the ladder. He squints and peers through the darkness, looking for Sunshine.

And then he remembers. He climbs down the ladder rapidly, trying not to remember. He sent Sunshine away. Sometimes he thinks she's back, just for a moment, but she's gone.

Downstairs the smell of smoke still hangs in the air. Lighter, but there. He can't see where it's coming from, though.

"What is it?" he asks his mother, who is putting on a heavy canvas slicker. It must be meant for rain, but it looks like the kind of thing a firefighter might wear.

"My island," she says. "My island is burning. Come."

He doesn't move. His feet are attached to the floor. "How?" he says. "Why?" He feels stupid, slow, as though he has just walked into the middle of a story and doesn't know which story he's in.

"I don't know how!" she exclaims. "Or why." She sounds angry now. Or maybe scared. "It could have been a lightning strike. I heard thunder."

She tosses him the life jacket he wore yesterday.

He catches it, holds it. What's he supposed to do with a life jacket in a fire?

It is then, standing there trying to understand, that he remembers . . . his campfire. Surely, though, that can't be the cause. He put it out before he left. He covered it with dirt, lots of dirt. The dirt had pine needles in it. Of course. There was no way to avoid the pine needles mixed with the dirt. But he stomped it real hard, and when he left, there wasn't even a thread of smoke.

Still, he started a fire. On his mother's island. Not far from here.

"Oh!" he cries. "Oh. I think I know—"

"No time for talk," she says, cutting him off. "Come with me. Hurry!" And she's out the door.

He follows, grateful to be forbidden to say what he thinks he knows.

When they step outside, the smoke assaults him. An egg-shaped moon rides high in the sky, giving enough light that he can see the smoke as well as smell it. It hangs over everything like the morning mist, but heavier than mist. Harsher. It bites his nose, claws at his throat when he breathes.

"Hurry!" his mother says again.

Where are they going? To the canoe? Are they going to paddle away and leave the island to burn?

He stumbles after her in the dark, his mind stumbling, too.

They arrive at the shore and his mother reaches under the canoe and hands him a paddle. Then, in one fluid motion, she flips the canoe over her head and walks with it into the water.

"Put on your life jacket!" she says, still in the

same sharp, clipped tone. She sets the canoe afloat and points to the stern bench.

He struggles into the life jacket, zips it closed, but he doesn't move toward the canoe. She wants him in the stern? The one in the stern steers!

"Hurry!" she says, for what feels like the hundredth time.

Ben gives up wondering. He just wades into the lake and climbs into the canoe, settles on the back bench. The smoke is growing thicker with every breath, but he still can't see flames.

His mother wades back to the shore and returns carrying a long, dark shape. She drops the object between his feet and ties a rope to the stern. "Paddle out fifteen or twenty feet," she says, "and then open the anchor and drop it in."

So she's sending him out onto the lake. Alone.

"Then what do I do?" he asks.

"When you get out there, you wait," she tells him. "Stay until I come back to signal that it's safe to return to shore."

Ben grips the paddle hard to stop his hands from shaking. His whole body is numb, wooden.

But he pokes the paddle into the lake and pushes. The canoe moves. Not far, but it moves.

"What if . . . ?" he turns back to ask, but he can't finish the sentence. *What if the fire gets you? What if you never come back to signal? What do I do then?*

"Wait until morning," she says, answering his unspoken question in that uncanny way she has. "If I don't come by morning light, go that way."

She points, not across to where the bears are, to where he paddled yesterday, but off to the right. "When you arrive at another shore, turn left and keep paddling. You'll come to a cabin. There are people there. They'll help."

"Shouldn't I go to the cabin now?" he asks. "Don't we need help now?"

"No. It's too dangerous in the dark. You'd never find it." She turns away, then back again. "Remember. Don't come unless I call you," she says. "I want you safe." And she disappears into the roiling smoke.

Ben sits for several beats, trying to discern a mother shape in the shifting dark. When he can't, can't see anything really, he grips the paddle and applies it to the water. How far is fifteen or twenty feet? He has no idea.

He paddles until the island feels farther away than he wants it to be, the smoke still too close, then he lays down the paddle and examines the anchor. It's not very heavy. It must be the arms, now folded closed, that make it work.

Open it, she said, so he opens it and lobs the spidery thing over the side. It plunges through the water pulling the rope after. When it stops, the canoe bobbles for a moment. Then everything goes still.

Ben takes a deep breath. The air is cleaner out here. The wind that was so blustery yesterday has mostly calmed, and the lake lies around him, still and black. The sky is a deeper black than he has ever seen in the city. Stars beyond counting stretch overhead. The stars shine back at him from the surface, too. He floats in a sea of stars.

He takes another long, wavering breath, filling his lungs, filling his whole body. Then he lets it out again very slowly.

The fire is his fault. Even if his mother doesn't know, he knows. Her going away is his fault, too. He's always known that.

She left because of him. Because of something he did. Something terrible.

He doesn't remember what it was. He's tried and tried to remember, and he can't.

But he knows he did it.

Chapter 14
Watching

Ben shivers.

He has no idea how long he's been sitting in the canoe watching the smoke. It crawls across the water like a hand reaching for him, pointing at him. He does know that in all that time, he hasn't cried once.

It's an emptying thing, crying, and sometimes a person needs emptying. But it doesn't change anything on the outside. Tears certainly can't put out a fire. They can't bring a mother back, either. He's known that almost as long as he's known anything.

Now he can see flames through the smoke, an

encroaching glow, low to the ground. It never seems especially fierce, though, not like a real forest fire. The trees themselves don't seem to be burning.

The smoke doesn't stay low the way the fire does. It rises and rises until even the stars disappear. The ones in the sky and, because those are gone, the ones on the water, too.

Still, the island is smoky and hot. And his mother is right in the middle of it.

In front of him near the shore an enormous tree begins to glow. It's burning up from the inside!

From time to time a breath of wind comes, stronger than the rest. It rocks the canoe, sets it tugging against the anchor. It makes the flames leap.

What is his mother doing anyway? She hasn't come down to the lake for water even once. Even if she doesn't want water, shouldn't she come to check on him?

He waits. He waits and watches and waits. His head grows wobbly on the stem of his neck, so heavy that from time to time it bobs forward, taking his whole body with it. He catches himself each time, though, and jerks upright again, his heart thundering.

He can't sleep. He *must not* sleep!

He mustn't fall out of the canoe, either.

He has to keep watch for his mother. It's his fault that she's living alone here on this island. He sent her away. Like he sent Sunshine away. He's never told anybody he knows that, though. Especially not his dad.

It would be hard to tell anyway, because he remembers so little.

Though surely whatever he did that day couldn't have been half as bad as what he's done now. Burning down his mother's island.

She thinks it was the lightning. But the lightning never came close last night. He would have heard thunder if it had, wouldn't he? And even if he tried to put out his campfire, tried really hard, it had to be the cause. This fire, this enormous, gobbling fire, happened because of him.

He wraps his arms around himself and rocks forward and back, forward and back.

A fresh gust of wind roughs up the surface of

the lake, sets the canoe dancing at the end of its anchor rope. For an instant the smoke swirls away, and he can see stars again.

The gust sets the encroaching fire dancing, too.

He shivers again. If Sunshine were here, she would curl in his lap to keep him warm. If only Sunshine were here.

"Sunshine!" he calls to the air.

But the air doesn't answer.

The glowing fire crawls. Climbs. Leaps. Fire seems to be everywhere.

What is his mother doing? Is she safe?

"Mommy!" Ben can hardly believe the cry came from him. When has he called anybody Mommy?

"Sunshine!" he calls again.

And though he hadn't really expected a response, either from his mother or his dog, something, something he can barely make out, is coming, moving toward the shore. At first it looks like a patch of low-running flame, reddish gold, just a glow. Not a solid thing at all. He can see right through it.

And yet the glow moves closer. He's beginning

to make out a shape. Flying ears, paws splaying happily in every direction, a long plumed tail.

Sunshine! It can only be his Sunshine! She's coming because he called!

Or maybe his mother sent her. Maybe his mother needs him. Maybe she sent Sunshine to get him because she needs help.

Working fast, Ben pulls up the anchor, hand over hand, and drops it with its arms still outstretched into the bottom of the canoe. Then he picks up the paddle and pushes hard, hard until the bow bumps into the shore.

His mother sent his daemon to get him!

When he's pulled the canoe safely onto the shore, Sunshine is there, wriggling, scrabbling, rising onto her hind legs. He leans over and she leaps into his arms. He holds her close.

She seems to have forgotten how mean he was to her just a little while ago.

He sets her down again, and she bows, her paws outstretched, her rump high, her eyes intent on his face. *Come with me!* those eyes say. *Come this way!*

And so Ben follows.

The base of the outhouse, when he passes it, is beginning to smolder, the flame crawling along the bottom logs. A sound bursts from him when he sees it, something between a giggle and a hiccup.

He slaps his hand over his mouth.

It's not funny. Nothing will ever be funny again.

When he steps into the clearing surrounding the cabin, he can make out a silhouette. The silhouette is bent over a shovel a short distance away from the cabin.

It's his mother. Of course. Sunshine runs up to her, and his mother pauses in her digging and bends over, reaching as though to take the little dog into her arms. When she unbends, though, Sunshine is gone. It's as though his dog disappeared into her arms, into her.

His mother straightens again and goes back to digging. It all happens so fast that it's almost as though it hasn't happened at all.

She stands on the spade, puts her full weight on it, jumps to press it into the rocky earth. Then she steps off, lifting away what she has loosened, throwing it behind her.

The quantity of root-bound, rocky soil she throws with each lift of the shovel isn't great, but she's fast. Almost before the dirt has landed, she's standing on the spade again, stepping off, throwing more.

Whatever she's doing, he wants to do it with her.

"Mom!" he cries, running toward her. "Let me help! Please!"

She has a kerchief tied over her nose and mouth, and all he can see of her face, the part above the kerchief, is black with soot.

"I want to help!" he says again.

For an instant, she stares at him, her eyes wide and startled. Then she says, "Ben, if anything happened to you, I'd never forgive myself."

"If anything happened to you—" he says, but he can't finish.

She peers into his face. She seems to be reading something there, something he doesn't try to hide. Then she takes off her kerchief and, without even asking, as though she has a mother's right, she ties it around his face. She points to a rake on the ground.

"Stay close by my side, but rake everything you can away from the house. We can't stop the island from burning, but maybe we can save the cabin."

She picks up her spade and goes back to digging.

Ben understands now. He drags the rake through brush, twigs, pine needles, pulling it all away from the log walls. His mother, working ahead of him, digs up weeds, small bushes, all that can burn. And everything she releases with her spade, he rakes away.

When a small point of the fire comes crawling, almost to their feet, his mother takes up an ax, goes to an evergreen tree at the edge of the clearing, and hacks off a branch. She uses the green branch like a broom to brush the burning material back toward the fire.

They work side by side without speaking, without stopping. Ben never pauses to consider whether his arms and back ache, whether the blisters on his hands from yesterday's paddling hurt like fury, whether his eyes burn and his throat and lungs sting. If he lets himself think about any of that, he will turn into a little kid again and be no use. So he ignores it all.

At last his mother straightens, tosses her spade away, and says, "Enough. Either the cabin will survive or it won't. We've got to get out of here."

Relief washing through him, Ben tosses the rake, too. It feels good to toss it, though his arms are so tired that the rake falls back almost at his feet.

They head together to the canoe. This time the flames have climbed higher on the hated outhouse and Ben laughs right out loud when he passes it, but his mother doesn't seem to notice . . . either the burning outhouse or his strange laughter.

Seeing the logs burn, though, he can't help but think about his mother's cabin. Will that burn, too? His laughter sputters and dies.

When they reach the lake, she doesn't flip the canoe over her head and walk it into the water the way she's done before. She just drags it in until it floats. Ben settles into the bow, and she climbs into the stern and paddles out a short distance. Then she turns the canoe so they are facing the island and drops the anchor.

They sit there together, watching her island burn.

CHAPTER 15
The End of the World

Ben grips the sides of the canoe and leans forward. "Look," he says, but his mother is already looking.

Before them on the shore, the crown of the enormous old tree that has been burning from inside has burst into flame. The blaze crackles and snaps and lights up the sky. Then, in the next puff of wind, the flame leaps to the crown of another tree nearby.

And then on to another.

Now the fire, which used to be only on the ground, travels from treetop to treetop, too.

"That's called a crown fire," his mother says.

She says it calmly, as though she's reading something from an encyclopedia.

Ben can hear his heart beating. At least he thinks that's what he's hearing. It's hard to be certain over the breathy roar of the fire.

If the sight of the burning island were not so terrible, it would be beautiful. The flames white-gold at the center, rising into orange, into red. Beautiful, though terrible still. He doesn't know how the two can exist at once, the beautiful and the terrible, but they do.

Ben turns to check on his mother. Her face, blackened entirely since she gave him her kerchief, is almost invisible in the smoky dark. Mostly he can see the whites of her eyes. He can't make out her expression. He looks away again. He's glad he can't see her expression.

At least she's here. She's safe.

They are safely here. Except for Sunshine. He has seen no trace of his little dog since she appeared on the shore and led him to his mother, since she leapt into his mother's arms.

"Did you see her?" he asks at last.

"Sunshine?"

"Yes. You sent her to get me. To tell me you needed help. But then she disappeared."

"I was thinking about you," his mother says. "Every minute. I kept wanting to go check on you, but there was no time. So maybe I did send Sunshine to you. Though I didn't mean for her to bring you into the fire."

"You needed me," he says.

"You were a great help," she says. She sounds like she means it, but her voice still carries no emotion.

Ben holds the thought close nonetheless.

The fire burns and burns. It flows along the ground and from crown to crown, too, in separate fires. More and more often, though, the ground fire and the crown fire meet in the center to consume an entire tree.

His fire. His beautiful, terrible fire.

The longer Ben watches the destruction before him, the more determinedly the confession he escaped offering earlier pushes up inside him. It's like needing to throw up after eating something bad.

He clenches his teeth, traps his tongue inside, but the words come anyway.

"It's my fault," he says at last. His voice seems to echo in the smoky air. *My fault! My fault!*

"What do you mean?"

He turns again to see his mother's face. Her gaze hasn't left the fire.

"When I came back—" He stops, takes a huge breath. There seems nothing to do but finish.

"When I came back after exploring," he says again, "I landed, but I was on another part of your island. I couldn't find the cabin. I was lost and I . . . I was scared. So . . ." He stops again. Then he lets it all come in a rush.

When his confession is done, when he's told her everything, about starting the fire, about putting it out, really trying to put it out, she says nothing. His words might have dropped into the lake and sunk there.

"When I left," he says again, "there wasn't even a bit of smoke!"

His eyes measure the length of canoe. She can't hurt him. They are too far out onto the lake for her to step into the water to reach him. Unless she crawls the distance in the canoe.

Strangely, he's not afraid. Just curious, as though whatever is going to happen will happen to somebody he barely knows, somebody he doesn't much care about.

His mother sits with her back straight, her chin lifted, her attention unwaveringly on the fire.

"Well," she says finally. "Well."

And then nothing more.

Ben jerks awake. He's scrunched on the floor of the canoe, his neck creased by the edge of the bow bench. How did he manage to fall asleep like that?

The sky is no longer a star-pricked black. It's navy blue, and all but the brightest stars have fled. The eastern horizon has turned to silver touched with the faintest blush of pink.

He closes his eyes again, trying to sort where he is, what has happened.

The island, his mother's island . . . gone.

Ben rubs his eyes, then opens them once more. His eyeballs feel gritty and his throat burns. When he lifts his head, his mother is watching from the canoe's stern.

Is she going to let him have it now? About going off in her canoe? About burning her island down?

But she says only, "Good morning."

When he answers, his voice rasps. "Good morning."

"It's time to go." She speaks calmly, as though "it's time to go" is an ordinary plan for any ordinary day.

He sits up, checks out the island. The fire still burns, but it is no longer raging. So many blackened tree trunks. The outhouse has burned to the ground.

But as the rim of sun peeks over the horizon, he can make out a dark square with a peaked roof beyond the burned trees. The cabin.

His mother's island is ruined, but her cabin stands. He hasn't destroyed that.

He can't say the same for Sunshine, though. She might as well have burned up in the fire. She didn't return even while he slept. His throat tightens.

He knows, of course, it's not possible for an

imaginary dog to burn up in a real fire. But maybe what happened is even worse. Maybe she burned up in his mind.

He's exhausted, despite his brief sleep. He's hollowed out like the tree he watched eaten by flames from the inside.

Now they will paddle back to town and his mother will make that call. She'll tell his dad that his son—their son—destroyed her island.

Does she know he destroyed Sunshine, too? Will she tell Dad that? His father won't feel bad about Sunshine's being gone, that's for sure.

Ben picks up the second paddle and dips it into the water. But with every thrust, he calls in the silence of his heart, *Sunshine! Sunshine! Sunshine!*

It's no use. The prow where the doggy figurehead once perched remains empty.

No wonder this feels like the end of the world. It is.

Chapter 16
Not Strong Enough to Stay

"Let's go to the café first." Ben's mother flips the canoe onto the beach and straightens slowly. "I know we're filthy, but I'm starving. You must be, too. We can get a room and a shower at the motel after we eat."

Her face is rimmed with soot. They tried to wash in the lake when they stopped to portage, but her skin is still gray and there's a darker line around the edges. He hasn't seen his own face, but it's probably little better.

Anyway, she's right. He is starving.

They settle at the Formica table in the same

booth where they had lunch with his dad so long ago. At least it feels long ago. So much has happened. But the same hamburger with French fries is still on the menu. He orders that.

He orders a root beer, too. He didn't ask for root beer when his dad was here. Dad says all that sugar rots the brain as well as teeth. But his mother won't care.

"Milk," she says to the waitress after he has placed his order. "He'll have milk."

Ben hates milk. He can't remember a time when he's been able to stand drinking it. At least not plain. At home his dad lets him put stuff in it to get it down—chocolate, peppermint oil, even chai tea. Just so it isn't *milk*.

He doesn't intend to start drinking it now, but he's too exhausted to argue. His mother must be exhausted, too. Across from him in the booth, she leans back against the cracked plastic upholstery and closes her eyes.

A toddler in the booth behind them pops up to peer over the back of the seat. Ben grins and holds his hands in front of his face then flaps them open for a game of peekaboo. The little boy trills with laughter and drops out of sight. Then he bounces right back up for more.

Ben does it again, and the toddler laughs even longer, louder.

So, of course, he does it again.

Ben's mother ignores the noise going on over her head.

The boy is still at it when their food arrives. The problem with little kids is that they don't know when to quit.

As Ben and his mother eat, flecks of ash keep falling from their hair and clothes onto everything on their plates. He keeps eating anyway.

Except for the milk. He doesn't touch the ash-sprinkled milk.

When they finish, his mother goes to call his dad, which makes Ben's stomach twist. He pushes the worry aside. It will be a few days before he sees his father. Dad will have time to get past the worst of his upset.

Ben drops one of his last French fries onto the

floor beneath the table. He knows there is no one down there, but there's nothing wrong with pretending.

Where does Sunshine go when she disappears anyway? To find a home in some other boy's heart?

The mother with the little kid leaves, tugging him behind her like a reluctant pull toy. He walks backward, grinning and waving.

Ben doesn't wave back. He doesn't have a wave left in him.

He stuffs the last French fry into his mouth, cold and limp, and concentrates on chewing to stop his chin from wobbling.

His mother returns and sits across from him again. "I've gotten a room at the motel," she says. "We can both shower so we won't scare your dad when he gets here this afternoon."

An electric current slams Ben upright. "You told him to come? But I'm supposed to be here for a week. You promised me a whole week!"

He's trying to keep from shouting, but his voice comes out pretty loud.

His mother frowns. "You want to stay? Now? The island is in ashes."

"It doesn't matter. Whatever you're going to do next . . . go back to clean up? I can help!"

Doesn't she understand anything?

But apparently she doesn't. "Ben," she says, "I don't want you back there in that mess. Smoke and soot are hard on the lungs. It would be even harder on your lungs than on mine because you're young." She shakes her head emphatically. "Besides, clearing all that burned stuff away. It wouldn't be any fun."

"Fun!" he cries. "I didn't come here to have fun!" He *is* shouting now, and two old men drinking coffee at the counter look over at them. He doesn't care, though. He doesn't care about anything. He's not giving up.

His mother's face creases into a quizzical frown. "Then why *did* you come?" she asks.

Why did he come? Why?

"Because . . ." he says. "Because," he says again. "Because," he says a third time. And then the rest comes in a rush. "I thought if you got to know me, the me I am now, not the little kid I used to be, maybe you'd want to come home with me. With me and Dad. Come home and stay."

She sits there, across from him, her eyes round with surprise. Her mouth round, too. Despite the coating of ash, her hair glows reddish gold under the electric lights. Hair that is the exact same color his little dog used to be.

Ben has never let himself see it before. If he made Sunshine up partly from the dog that used to live next door, he made her up even more from his absent mother.

And now he's losing both of them. Sunshine is gone. He can't call her up any longer. And his mother won't come home with him. He can tell by the way she's looking at him, so astonished at the idea, that she won't.

She says nothing, though, so he adds, "I know when I was a little kid I did something bad. Something that made you go away. But I'm diffcrent now. I was going to show you how different I am.

So you'd want me. So you'd want to be my mother. Again."

He's run out of words. Out of hope, too. The whole idea was stupid to start with. And he's messed everything up anyway. All the things he did wrong. Shrugging her hand away, running when she told him not to run, taking off in her canoe.

Burning her island down.

Why would she want him?

For just an instant, his mother looks as though she might laugh, and he can feel the first bubble of anger expanding in his chest. But whatever the impulse was that looked like laughter is gone as fast as it came.

Instead, she reaches a hand across the table, exactly the way she reached for his dad that first day. Not touching, just reaching. And she says, "Oh, Ben. Oh, my dear Ben. I'm so sorry."

But he cares nothing about sorry.

She keeps sitting there, keeps looking at him. Her hand keeps reaching.

"How much do you remember about the day I left?" she asks.

He pulls back into the corner of the booth, as far away from that reaching hand as the enclosed space allows. "Not much," he mumbles.

That's not exactly true, though. He does remember . . . something. Scraps float up from time to time. A red truck. A glass of milk. A tall glass filled with milk. The glass falling, breaking. Milk and shards of glass everywhere.

"Milk," he says at last. "Did I spill some milk?"

And even though that scrap of memory has been there forever, he's still surprised when she nods. "That's right," she says. "You spilled a glass of milk."

A tiny shudder ripples beneath Ben's skin.

She withdraws her hand, drops it into her lap. "It was lunchtime," she says, looking down at her lap as though she's just discovered something very interesting there. "An ordinary lunchtime. I'd spent the whole morning cleaning the kitchen, and I had it spotless. It didn't mean a thing to me, keeping stuff so clean, but you know how your dad is."

Ben nods. He knows.

"Anyway," his mother says, "you were playing

with one of those little cars of yours. Do you remember those little cars you used to have?"

Ben nods again. His Matchbox cars. He still plays with them sometimes, though they're jumbled in a box in the back of his closet now.

"You brought one of them to the table. I told you not to, but you did. You took them everywhere those days. And you were running it across the table—"

"The fire truck," Ben says. "It was the red fire truck."

"Yes. I think you're right. The fire truck. And you bumped it into the glass of milk I had waiting there. It was a tall glass, because you loved milk."

I loved milk?

"I must have set it down too close to the edge of the table, and you bumped the little car, the little fire truck, into the glass and knocked it right off the table—"

"And it smashed," Ben says. "Milk everywhere. And glass . . ."

"Everywhere," his mother finishes. She picks up

her coffee, brings it to her lips, sets it down without tasting it. She's looking at him now.

"And I . . ." The gold-flecked eyes hold him. "It was no big deal, Ben. Just a glass of milk. 'Don't cry over spilled milk,' they say. 'Spilled milk' stands for everything that doesn't matter, everything you're supposed to let go of once it's happened. But I . . ."

"You grabbed me out of my chair and you looked at me like . . ." Ben closes his eyes. He remembers the snatching. He remembers dangling with his feet off the floor, hands holding. Even when he forgot the face, couldn't call back even the color of his mother's hair, he still remembered that look.

"Like I was going to hurt you."

"I was scared," he says.

"I know," she answers. "I know."

She breathes in, filling herself, then letting the air out again very slowly. "I saw how scared you were, and I hated myself for your scared. I didn't want you to feel like that ever again. Not about me. Not about anything. And I loved you, loved you so much . . . but I knew then that I couldn't be trusted. Couldn't trust myself. Some hurt place inside me kept wanting to hurt in return."

She laughs, but it's clear this time the laugh's not at him. It's a small, dry hiccup of a laugh. Aimed at that hurting place inside herself.

"Such a little thing," she adds, after the laugh has dribbled away. "Spilled milk."

"And so you took me over to Mrs. Schwartz, and I stayed there and played with her dog."

His mother nods. "I took you to Mrs. Schwartz. I told her an emergency had come up, and I asked her if you could stay until your daddy got home. And then I . . . left. Because I knew I just . . . couldn't . . . do it. I'd known for a long time, really. But that day I knew for sure."

They both sit there, looking at one another across the table.

"At least," she says finally, "you still have Sunshine."

When Ben tries to speak, tears come instead of words. He had such hopes. And he's spoiled it. Spoiled it all.

Even Sunshine. He's even spoiled Sunshine.

"What?" his mother asks. "What is it?"

And so he explains. The tossed pebbles. Ordering Sunshine to leave. How she did what he said.

He tells her how Sunshine came back during the fire, looking like low-running flame. How she led him to where his mother was digging around the cabin. How he hasn't seen her since.

His mother listens.

"Oh, Ben," she says when he's done. Nothing more. Just *Oh, Ben.* And then, "Maybe she isn't gone. Surely you'll dream about her now and then. I think she'll come back to you in your dreams."

Ben shakes his head, but it's an automatic response, refusing comfort because he doesn't deserve comfort.

Maybe, though, he *will* dream of Sunshine. He'd like that.

His mother goes silent again. After a time she says, "I've been thinking and thinking about it. I'm pretty sure your campfire didn't start the fire. You did what you should have done to put it out. Exactly. And last night there was a lightning strike soon after we went to bed. Really close. You must have heard it."

Ben shakes his head. He didn't hear it. He's not sure he believes she did, either.

"A lightning strike without any rain. And everything has been so dry. That must be how the fire started."

"But you can't be sure," he says. "You can't!"

He doesn't know why he's arguing. Why can't he just be glad she's not blaming him?

His mother shrugs. "No," she says. "I can't be sure. But neither can you. I think most likely it was the lightning, and I think you and I should both put the whole matter behind us."

Put the whole matter behind us. Ben considers that. "Then," he says, "then, you forgive me? Even if my campfire *might* have burned your island, you really forgive me?"

She nods. "I forgive you, Ben." She says it simply, forcefully. But then she spoils it by adding "Do you think you will ever be able to forgive me?"

The question stops him cold. Will he? Will he

ever be able to forgive the mother who left that three-year-old boy behind?

He studies her across the table—her hair, her eyes, her soot-grimed face. This time he's going to remember her face. If he never sees his mother again, he's going to remember.

But forgive her? He doesn't answer. He can't.

"I know I have no right to ask," she says. "I've had years and years to do it, but I haven't forgiven my mother still. I think *I* would be different if I'd been able to."

"Your mother used to hit you," Ben says, remembering.

"Yes," his mother says. "And more."

Ben tries to imagine being hit . . . and more. He can't really.

"But I want you to know, Ben, I try. I've forgiven some of the smaller things. Like how she'd leap out from behind a door and yell 'BOO!' Used to make me jump out of my skin. Make me cry, too. She was just trying to play. I know that now. And she didn't know how. I've forgiven her that."

His mother ducks her head, then lifts it slowly until she's looking straight at him. "Maybe there's something little you can forgive me, just for a start."

Ben draws his finger through the smear of ketchup on the plate in front of him. It's the only thing left on the plate except for a scattering of ash.

"Ever since you left," he says, "I've been scared. Not 'boo!' scared, but worried-that-bad-things-are-going-to-happen scared. Dad calls me 'the what-if kid.'"

"Yeah," his mother says very softly. "Yeah," she says again. "A little kid losing his mother. That would be enough to make you scared."

She pauses then as though she's waiting for him to accuse her further, but he can find nothing else to say. Just that one thing—"I've been scared"—seems to have emptied him out.

She leans toward him then and speaks in a low, earnest voice. "You haven't been a what-if kid here, Ben. You asked to come. You were going to spend a whole week on my island with me even though I'm nearly a stranger to you. You climbed that ladder. You slept in my dark loft."

So she knows that he's afraid of the dark, too. He never told her that.

Her mouth quirks. "You even went off on your own in my canoe."

Heat floods his face. Embarrassment for sure. But maybe pride, too. He did do all those things. He did!

At last he smiles. "I guess I can forgive you for being tired of cleaning the kitchen," he says.

She smiles, too, but then turns solemn again. "And yourself?" she asks. "Can you forgive yourself?"

"Forgive myself?" he asks.

That nod again. "For being three years old? For bringing your fire truck to the table? For having a mother you couldn't keep?"

"For spilling my milk?" he adds.

"For spilling your milk," she says.

He's never thought of forgiving himself . . . for anything. He nods, too, and that seems to be enough.

His mother heaves herself to her feet. "Let's go," she says. "I don't know about you, but I want a nap after that shower."

It's when she is standing across from him that Ben notices again what he saw when she first arrived. How small his mother is. She can lift a canoe onto her shoulders and carry it to the next lake, but she's not much taller than he is. Small but strong.

Not strong enough to stay, though.

Not strong enough to stay.

When he is on his feet, too, something tells him to walk the short but oh-so-long distance from one side of the booth to the other to give his mother a hug.

He doesn't do it, though.

CHAPTER 17
Next Summer

They stand beside the car. Ben's father jingles the keys in his pocket. His mother scuffs at the dirt with the toe of a sneaker.

To Ben's surprise, his dad hasn't given him the lecture. The one about "being responsible," about "thinking before you act." Not yet anyway. He'll probably deliver it on the way home.

It doesn't matter. Ben knows that lecture by heart. Maybe he'll even listen this time. While they're driving home. Without his mother. Without Sunshine.

"Well," Dad says after the silence has stretched

nearly to the breaking point. He lays a hand, warm and familiar, on Ben's back. "I guess we'd better get going."

Ben can smell shaving lotion. His dad shaved. Again. Even though he had to hurry to get here.

"It's a long drive," his mother says. "It'll be late when you get home."

Still no one moves.

They go on standing there, looking at one another, looking away. Looking at one another again.

Even his mother's freckles have gone pale.

Dad jingles his keys some more.

Ben waits for his mother to leave first. That's the way they do it in their family. She leaves first. But instead she steps closer and presses a palm to his chest. The hand covers his heart.

"Remember, Benny," she says, "Sunshine is right there. Always will be."

Then she smiles at them both—the saddest smile Ben has ever seen, but a smile—and turns away.

Ben stands watching the forlorn slope of her shoulders, the firmness of her step.

"Wait!" he calls. "Mom, please, wait."

She stops. Waits. But she doesn't turn to look at him.

"Next summer," he says to her waiting back. "Can I come visit next summer?"

When she pivots, her face is lit from within. "You really want to?" she asks.

Ben checks the feeling expanding inside him.

"Yes," he says. "I really want to."

Light dances in her smile. "You'll love the island next summer!" Her words come in a rush. "It will be so different than it is now. Everything will be growing. You'll see. Not big trees, of course, but flowers, saplings, so much more. And I . . . I will be so glad to see you."

Ben runs and throws his arms around her. She holds him for a long time.

Just as he steps back out of the hug, he notices it. A firm pressure against his leg, a kind of leaning. He looks down and there she is. Right where she's supposed to be. Where she's always been.

Sunshine!

He reaches down to lay his hand on the hard

little skull, to run a furry ear through his fingers. When he straightens again, his mother is waiting, watching.

"What if . . ." he says very quietly. "What if I leave my daemon here? With you. To keep you company until I come back."

His mother's eyes widen. "Is she here again?"

He nods.

She looks at the ground by his feet, looks directly at the small dog waiting there. "Do you think Sunshine would stay with me?" she asks.

"If you want her. I know she will."

Sunshine wags her long plumed tail.

"Okay," his mother says. "Sure. We'll be waiting for you then. Both of us will be here waiting. Next summer."

She pats her leg to call the little dog to her side, and this time when she walks away, Sunshine follows.

Ben watches them both. He stands there so long, perfectly still, that his father comes up beside him.

"Are you ready to go home?" Dad asks, wrapping an arm around his shoulders and pulling him close.

Ben leans into the hug. Yes. He's ready. To go home. With his father.

Still . . . his heart is singing.

Next summer!

Next summer!

ACKNOWLEDGMENTS

For reasons known only to the story itself, the process of creating *Sunshine* turned out to be a long one. So many friends—good writers, good readers—read and read and read the manuscript, suggested and encouraged and suggested and encouraged again, that I dare not list you here. If I tried I would, inevitably, miss some who were important to the long process. So I ask you to name yourself here and to know you had my gratitude at the time and you have it still.

But I must call out JoAnn Bren Guernsey, who read more times than any friendship had a right to expect; Eugenie Doyle, whose wisdom I have so often relied on; and Ellen Howard, who put her gentle finger on the snag that almost kept this story from its true resolution. Thank you to each of you. Thank you.

And thank you, of course, to Rubin Pfeffer, the agent I never thought I needed until I was gathered into his fold, and Liz Bicknell, the perfect editor to bring my late-career books into the world.